PRAISE FOR THE BOOK

'A fantastically vivid reimagining of a classical society in which life is neatly ordered and culturally sophisticated but also uncertain, violent and dramatic. Kuroor has drawn characters distinctly modern in their troubled self-consciousness, driven to seek not the heroic destinies celebrated in legends but highly personal and recognizable ends.'

Anjum Hasan, author of *History's Angel*

'A great novel in the tradition of O.V. Vijayan's *Legends of Khasak*. A writer who left me amazed. A madness seems to have possessed Manoj Kuroor. A novel such as this is rare indeed.'

Jeyamohan, author of *Stories of the True*

'Manoj Kuroor's *Nilam Poothu Malarnna Naal* is a rare work in Indian literature. It takes a language as its theme, philosophy and metaphor. Before it was consecrated and confined in the stone idols of Sanskrit by the anthanar – the brahmins – and the varathar – the ones who came from elsewhere – the Malayalam language was rooted in the fertile soils of the Dravida tongue. There it thrived and flourished and bloomed lushly. *Nilam Poothu Malarnna Naal* brings back to life that experience and marks it in our memory. The book is a reverent song resplendent with the fiery sparks that flew off the history of the ancient people of Kerala and the politics that shaped it. This narrative of the tribal life of yore is such that it makes possible a pan-Indian moulting of the caste system and the history of languages.

I believe this book is a milestone in the history of Malayalam literature. Only someone like Manoj Kuroor who combines academic knowledge and creative imagination in language and literature, and scholarship with performance of music, is capable of such a feat – of imagining and realizing such a book.

It is also a milestone in the history of translation. For this is a book in which the translator inevitably encounters every single hurdle in the way of translation with the same intensity. It calls for deep knowledge of history, extraordinary mastery of language and the willingness to let the spirit be consumed by the soul of the work. This is a dangerous, risky dance on fire, of the text and translation, a great trance, and only J. Devika is capable of it.'

K.R. Meera, author of *Hangwoman*

'The great poets of ancient Tamil and the warrior-kings they praised or cursed inhabit the pages of Manoj Kuroor's exceptional, lyrical work. But this book is not a historical novel. It is a shimmering prose-poem, keyed to the natural world of southern India as it once must have been, or as a brilliant poet could reimagine it. Here the outer world of flowers, rivers, sky, wilderness, elephants, serpents and goddesses reflects the intense inner life of the characters, as if we were reading a compelling, classical Tamil poem composed just for us.'

David Shulman, author of *Tamil: A Biography*

THE DAY THE EARTH BLOOMED

Manoj Kuroor

Translated by J. Devika

B L O O M S B U R Y
NEW DELHI • LONDON • OXFORD • NEW YORK • SYDNEY

BLOOMSBURY INDIA
Bloomsbury Publishing India Pvt. Ltd
Second Floor, LSC Building No. 4, DDA Complex, Pocket C – 6 & 7,
Vasant Kunj, New Delhi 110070

BLOOMSBURY, BLOOMSBURY INDIA and the Diana logo
are trademarks of Bloomsbury Publishing Plc

Originally published in Malayalam as *Nilam Poothu Malarnna Naal*
by DC Books 2015
First published in India 2024
This edition published 2024

Copyright © Manoj Kuroor, 2024
English translation copyright © J. Devika, 2024

Manoj Kuroor has asserted his right under the Indian Copyright Act to be identified
as the Author of this work

ISBN: PB: 978-93-56407-43-5; e-ISBN: 978-93-56406-61-2
2 4 6 8 10 9 7 5 3 1

Typeset in Fournier MT Std by Manipal Technologies Limited
Printed and bound in India by Thomson Press India Ltd

To find out more about our authors and books, visit www.bloomsbury.com and sign
up for our newsletters

There were more than forty women poets writing in the Sangam era, their names mentioned with their songs in the anthologies. This book is dedicated to them.

CONTENTS

The Beginning

To the north, the hill of Venkada. To the south, the cape of Kumari. To the east and west, the boundless ocean. And in the middle – many, many places teeming with life, nestling in the heart of the mountains, valleys, woods, hills, lush fields and paddies, the dry wildernesses, the banks of rivers and the beaches by the sea. Lands big and small, with capricious borders. Aiynar and Kuravar, hunters; Uzhavar, farmers; Aayar, herders; Maravar, bandits who, however, were also warriors; Ummanar, salt makers; and Parathavar, fisherfolk. They lived and worked in their own nooks and niches on this expansive land. There were many other kinds of people too in these lands – singers, Paanar; dancers, Koothar; performers of Veriyaattam, Velar; silk weavers, Chaliyar; makers of the yaazh and the parai, Kuyiluvar; and doers of worship, Anthanar.

Seventeen centuries ago! Back then, the Exalted Three – the Chera, the Chozha and the Pandya – lorded over the larger dominions. They ruled sometimes in harmony, sometimes in discord. The land trembled when they plunged into clamorous war. Sometimes they came together to capture smaller territories.

Though not as bold as their overlords, the rulers and chieftains, Chittarayar and Kurunilamannar, and the minor landlords, Velkal, did not lack pluck. They too challenged each other time and again. They stole cattle when in need of wealth. Killed elephants. Reduced to ashes the fields of the fallen.

The Pulavar and Paavalar sang high praise of the victors. Radiant in the glow of their extravagant words, the rulers bestowed upon them gold and land. Some showered so much wealth on the singers and dancers that they came to be known by the name Vellal. Rulers believed that their lives were futile if the great song-makers, Perumpaavalar, did not celebrate them in words and music. Indeed, once, one such hero, filled with the fury of combat, declared: 'If I do not defeat my foes, let my name and my lands remain unsung by the Perumpaavalar, let them sink into gloom and oblivion!'

The wordsmiths, too, knew that showering praise on the powerful was the only way to become wealthy. When the rulers fought, some of them became mediators. Even spies, at times. But there were at least a few who dared to refuse, when the acts of the rulers turned ugly. The verses welded together by these different songmakers are etched on palm leaves as *Ettuthogai*, *Pathuppaattu* and *Pathinenkeezhkkanakku*. They became famous later as the Songs of Koodal – *Koodalppaattu* – and the Songs of Ancient Tamizh.

There were others, besides these famed ones. People who could have put down roots in many places, but who were alone in the end. People who wandered together over long paths, but could not find a place of rest and growth. People who possessed no marks of renown, their lives tucked into collective nouns referring to the community they were part of; those who turned their very lives into words. You will not find their names in the Songs of Koodal, which brought power and glory to the lords of the land and the lords of verse. But their presence lingers in some lines, sometimes between the lines. Everything that they knew through their senses – colours, sights, sounds, smells and flavours. Like Malayalam, which stayed unwritten though many spoke it from long ago; it has its inner and outer worlds. This is their writing. Writing that was not imprinted on palm-leaf pages or mud tablets.

I
Kolumban

One

We were getting ready to leave – we did not know if we would return. We did not mull over that possibility among ourselves. If the algae broods over its loosened roots, it can never glide on a current. Ants in their anthills would not grow wings if they feared the moment of descent to the ground.

What is the point of travelling when all you know is about your immediate surroundings! And there wasn't much one knew, anyway. We lived near the forests, but we did not know how to hunt. There were fields of millet behind our huts, but we were unused to sowing and reaping, unlike the kuravar and uzhavar. But there were some things that we did know. We knew the drying stream in summer, the remnant of what was once a playful and feisty waterfall which bounced on and leapt from each mighty rock that lined its path from the top of the hill to the bottom. It shows a cheek stained with dried tears. We know when we see it – a river that dwells on the memory of how it flowed unfettered before it shrank and shrivelled. It too, like us, had a past of dance and music, a time in which it danced and sang and lived off this without a care. But that which is first taken in through the eye or ear, then swirled in one's heart and is reborn in dance or verse or song – that does not count as knowledge, does it?

The harsh summer of endless want was over. The rain began to fall fitfully. Whatever the omens, we had to begin our journey. We changed out of our garments woven from leaves into loincloths of cotton, covered our heads with cotton headgear and set out. Our clothes were in tatters. The women decked themselves with stone necklaces and bangles. Those ornaments too bore signs of wear. Many in our group were busy unpacking the things we needed for our dances and songs, tapping them to check their sounds.

High above, the rainclouds had massed, cutting off daylight. Thunder rang like the resonant booming of well-tightened muzhavu and aakulippara drums in unison. Flashes of lightning fell hard, again and again, on our little bronze cymbals, their light splitting and scattering on our hands, cheeks and eyes in a bright shower of drops. First, periyaazh – the big lute of the long strings – adorned with peacock feathers. The horns – kombukal – like the upraised trunks of elephants; the eyes of their bamboo bodies pierced at intervals to make small sound-holes. Then the theenguzhal, pipes. Firm-mouthed drums, the ellarippara, and then the pathalappara. We gathered together the yaazh with their strings loosened, and our other instruments, into cloth bundles. Hanging them on curved kavadi poles, we lifted them to our shoulders. The koothar dancers joined us, also carrying bundles hung on poles. On one side of the poles were their ellari and aakuli drums, thatta and kuzhal pipes, and on the other the muzham and thoomb. The bundles hung heavy on our shoulders, like the bulky fruit of the jack tree. The curved poles jerked and trembled with each step we took. The lowing sounds of bovine beasts rose from the leather bodies of our drums as they bumped against each other inside our bundles. The gentle sobbing of trees lingered in the hollows of the flutes.

We were on a mountain path. In a short interval between heavy spells of rain. The raging waters plunged down with vigour from the heights of the Elephant Peak, the Aanamala. Muddied, swirling currents shot out of the crevices on the mountain's rocky face. Its massive head quivered like a mighty elephant in musth, the thick liquid of passion flowing down the sides of its head. The gushing waters disappeared into the greenish darkness of the lush treetops and flowed down, down, until they fell upon the valleys and spread out in them. Above the curving, festive kavadi poles of the mountains and the forests rose the largest of them, the seven-hued curved kavadi of the sky.

'Anna, the rain is coming back!'

My little daughter Cheera shouted to her brother without taking her eyes off the sky. She skipped along, hanging on her mother's arm. Nellakkili and I have four children. Our eldest boy, Mayilan, left our home and this place early. Chithira is our second child, a daughter. Then a boy, Ulakan, and finally, Cheera. Cheera is closer to Ulakan than to her sister. She is always announcing something like this. But Ulakan, who was treading carefully on the slippery rock-path, holding on to the hands of the other children, probably did not hear her. Though not a child, he is playful. I usually hold my tongue when it wants to lash out at him.

'Nothing to fear,' I told her, looking at the sky. 'The aiynar's huts are just a little way off.'

The drizzle grew stronger. The yaazhs packed in the cloth bundles began to flirt with the raindrops. Though we tried to cover them with leaves and cloth and hold them closer, we could not hide their strings from the pitter-patter. The raindrops flowed on the bundles seeking out slits and chinks in their thin coverings.

Ahead, the huts made of eacha leaves appeared. They were oblong, like porcupines with bodies sheathed in quill coats, tails stretching behind. We and our padinis, our women, hurried behind our Perumpaanan, our leader, towards the huts; the koothar and their women, the viralis, came with us. The aiynar women heard us come. One of them who had been lying on a deerskin bed nursing her child got up and came out. Another woman had been gathering grass seeds from the ground; they fell off her lap and scattered on the ground. Yet another had been cooking ground grass seeds; she heard the noise and came over. A fourth woman had been drawing water from the well when we reached. She too was drawn out by the bustle. She stood on the path gazing at us, forgetting what had to be done at home, getting wet in the rain.

'We are paanar who sing and koothar who dance. We are on our way to a foreign land,' our Perumpaanan announced, not addressing anyone in particular. He was an excellent singer. He excelled at playing the yaazh too. If only there were people to listen, his voice would sound as though it rose from deep within, and not just from his throat. But now he sounded hoarse, like a wet yaazh.

One by one, the women came out of their huts.

'The rain is getting stronger. Can we please have a place to rest a while?'

The women looked astonished. Their eyes fell on the bony bodies of our children.

'Come in . . .'

Our children followed them in. They sat cross-legged on the floor. In a short while, the women laid out teak leaves in front of them. A meal! Their eyes sparkled. Their tongues grew moist and little springs spurted in their mouths. Their hands trembled. The rice and the roasted fish served on the leaves vanished in the snap of a finger. Their mothers sought to stop them, but their reproaches withered before they could reach their lips. Disapproving looks still flew from them towards the children. The little ones pretended not to see. For a brief while at least, dance and music and such things were but meaningless sound and twitchings of the body to them. Our children hunted with their hearts. They seized the prey with their teeth. Not meeting their mothers' pointed stares, their eyes roamed on the many kinds of grass that grew on the outer walls of the huts and on the elephant tusks mounted on the walls inside.

Next was our turn. The meal was of arrack brewed from fermented rice, rice, the cooked flesh of the monitor lizard and roast pork. Our growling bellies snatched each prey and cooked them in the heat of our inner juices. The children laughed to see how we gobbled and gulped our food. We were reminded once again of the sole antidote to hunger. We did not meet their eyes; we cringed in front of their swelling laughter.

By then the aiynar men had begun to return, carrying the hares they had caught on their hunt. The hunting dogs followed them, barking and announcing their return. The dogs kept leaping at the hares which hung on the men's shoulders. Hand us the fruits of our labour directly, they seemed to clamour, it is we who hunted them! But the hunters did not give in to the dogs' outcry. When the hunting party drew closer to the huts, the dogs' barking was directed at the visitors.

Their families told the party about us; the hunters chained the dogs. They hung their arrows and quivers on the walls. Covered the flasks of arrack with lids and pushed them under the cots. Those flasks – they must have got them when they exchanged the cows they stole in a cattle raid with the chantor, makers of liquor. We had heard of that. The aiynar soon turned the meat from their hunt that day into food for a feast.

The lightless day ended. Now darkness thickened over the sullen air. The heavy downpour eased somewhat. We knew that we could not travel in the dark; still, when the rain eased a little, we offered to leave – only to be generously stopped by them. They were to go that night to hunt the wild boar which came to drink the water collected in the footprints the deer leave in the mud. They postponed that for us, their guests.

The aiynar built warm fires in front of their huts. Bamboo cups brimmed with strong spirits brewed from honey. They served us cooked porcupine meat and ghee rice. They were sharing all that they had with us! Our eyes welled up with gratitude. We searched our bundles for something that we could give in return for their kindness that had given us a place to rest.

'Kolumba . . .'

I knew why Perumpaanan was calling me. I unpacked the periyaazh with twenty-one strings. It looked like an incomplete female body. I had named it Mallika years back, in the hope that it would actually turn into a woman.

Mallika was all decked up, as pretty as a peacock. Then I brought the other lutes and drums out of the bundles. I tightened their threads. The instruments hummed and came alive. Soon, pitch-perfect sounds rose from them. The drums accompanied them. The music from our throats flowed out in waves. It soared right up to the heights of the dark foliage above and echoed back. The hunters picked up their drums too. The sounds that made the leather bodies of the drums tremble leapt out. They threw open the frail confinements of the leafy barriers around us and wandered about in the open.

The full moon rose. The viralis, who wore garlands of jasmine that shone like abundant moonlight, shook open their ample tresses and began to dance. They were like small trees shaking in the wind. Chithira and Cheera too danced as they sang. The koothar were dancing along. There was no one even in faraway lands, after all, who could best Chanthan in dancing the koothu. As usual, something tugged hard inside at the sight of Chithira and Chanthan dancing together. Like a thorn prick, inside. I had set much store by Chanthan. Many a time I had thought that he was trying to cosy up to Chithira. They danced in abandon; now they were dancing with passion, like mating snakes. But then I thought, maybe not. I am just letting my worry grow. I know Chithira and Chanthan. They were just lost in dance, maybe. As the koothaattam stretched on, many fell asleep in the open ground in front of the huts, exhausted.

I sat down, leaning on an ilavu tree. I had merely made a show of joining in the singing and dancing; I could only step back and stay put in a corner. Cheera, who had been singing loudly till then, was now drained; she lay asleep near Ulakan. Chithira was with them. My mind cooled, noticing that Chanthan was elsewhere. I sat there, gazing at each sleeping body. The flowers that had adorned the girls' hairdos were scattered all over the ground. Their fading scent, the waning moon and the sleepers made me drift into a doze.

'Asleep?'

I opened my eyes. It was Velan. He was among those who had so enthusiastically served us food; an aiynan. He smiled soundlessly, like a flower blooming in the dark night.

'Didn't sleep. Just wanted to sit here, leaning . . .'

'Why didn't you join in the dancing and singing?'

'Aren't we on our way somewhere? I am in a hurry to find what we seek.'

'You are trying to get away from hunger, aren't you? Why be sad during these little moments of respite?'

'Not just that, my friend. This time, I am going in search of my son, too. He left when he was very young. As for hunger, it is the only store that we have ever had. He wanted to escape it. I'll join the maravar – make war or loot – and end this state of ever-growing want, he used to say. And then, one day, he slipped away without a word to anyone.'

'Is that so? Where will you search for him? Do you have any clue where he may be?'

'Someone from the paana group that travels the lands told me that he was seen in the land of a chief called Nannan. This was long ago. My girl Chithira wasn't grown then. Cheera wasn't born . . . And I must also find a patron and end our hardship.'

'Why didn't you seek your son till now?'

'I thought about it many times. Then set it aside. Let him at least not share our indigence, we thought. Would we stop him if he managed to get back on dry land somehow? If he found refuge?'

Velan's hand grasped my shoulder.

'Friend, be at peace. Your wish will come true. Now, sleep. Rest.'

I had been sitting there leaning on the tree, unable to sleep. But sometime in the night, my tired eyes closed.

Two

The day dawned. I woke up with a start and saw that I wasn't leaning on the tree any more. Because the falling leaves piling steadily on the ground were thick as a mattress, slumber on it felt like a light, slow, gentle descent from the skies above. As soon as I got up, I woke the others. They too scrambled up. The children were also roused from their tired slumber. We made haste. The padini and virali women adorned their hair with the golden-coloured blossoms of the venga tree. The aiynar took pains to warn us about the possible dangers ahead. The radiance of a moonlit night and abundant kindness had so sated us, we struggled with the tides of warmth that swelled in our hearts which were too immense to be poured out as words. The more I wiped my eyes, the more they welled. Before the day grew brighter, we bid goodbye to the aiynar and turned back to the road.

The mountain path lay soaked in last night's rains, shiny and slippery, like a python.

'How I wish we could stay here and be hunters,' whispered Cheera to her mother. 'Better than singing songs!'

Nellakkili threw me a wry smile. Hidden in it were many thorns. I, who recited the Arathupaal, the Way of Dharma, from the *Thirukkural*, whenever she talked about our poverty, was their target. Not a single day passed without mention of our distress. Mallika was my refuge in those difficult hours. I would run my fingers over her veins.

Those who seek refuge in Him
who is unswayed by want and non-want
Never will they be harrowed by misery

Those lines would make Nellakkili curl her fingers and clench her fists hard, trying to suppress the anger that blazed in her. Precisely at such moments, Cheera would pipe up in all innocence: 'Acha, the song you wrote – "Close the body's doors, listen to the inmost" – can you sing it please?'

Nellakkili would thump the walls with her fists in sheer frustration. Chithira would evade her mother's eye and throw me a secret smile.

'Not that one. I'll sing another.' Mallika would throb again.

> *If she has beauty*
> *Then what does she lack?*
> *If she lacks beauty*
> *Then what does she have?*

Cheera may or may not know their meaning, but she was in love with songs. Now she too rejects them.

'The path is slippery, little ones, heed! You will fall!' Perumpaanan called out.

'Amma, our puppies must be dead now?'

Though she did not ask about them often, I knew that they were on Cheera's mind all the time. If I looked into her eyes, my own would grow moist. That dog, which had come back to be with us though we had turned her away, had given birth just two days ago in our crowded hut. The pups had not yet opened their eyes. Their little mouths sought their mother's teats, but they were quite dry. Our tame dog – our poverty had dripped onto her. Unable to let flow into her teats the tenderness she felt for little ones, she kept moaning. Cheera forgot her hunger as she sat at a distance watching the pups intently. They still reeled in the shock of being born into this world without sustenance or succour and scampered blindly between their mother's legs.

Nellakkili had no time to gaze at them. The knowledge that the bellies of her loved ones burned with hunger must have turned her mind away from greater kindnesses. Ulakan and I were wiping off the mould from the leather surfaces of the drums. For a moment, she fixed us with a cold stare. Then she stepped out to cut some wild greens. She tore them, threw them into the water boiling on the hearth and closed the pot. When the leaves changed colour, she picked up the salt pot and felt its insides thoroughly, even though she knew that it was empty. There was no money in the box to give the umanar when they brought salt. We learned that all unsalted food tasted the same.

I did not feel like staying back at home. And so I had gone out. Though I spent some time chatting in paana homes where the singing had dried up, no one told each other of their neediness. But we all knew about each other. Maybe everyone felt that all that was once ours had been washed away; and what we possessed now was becoming useless. This was probably why Chanthan's voice had grown louder amidst the whispered conversations.

'Are we to live forever having nothing?' he asked. 'We must leave. Or we will have to see each of us die one by one. Just remember all those who passed away recently. Though their loved ones will never say that they died of hunger, don't we know the truth? Why did Mayilan go away from this place?'

Chanthan had been Mayilan's playmate. His mother had died giving birth to him. He was now grown up, but his father had died during one of those days of famine we had endured. I remember Mayilan each time I see Chanthan. And when he sees me, he probably remembers his childhood friend. He had not noticed me in this group, most likely. But when he saw me, his voice faltered. Remembering my old friend who had given him life, I lowered my head. After Mayilan left, I continued to live, but with the feeling that my body had been cleaved in two; it was as if one half of it hung detached. Nellakkili would weep for him almost every day back then. After a while, she too fell silent. I knew that my sorrow was growing heavy, like water filling in a dam, and so I kept quiet, knowing well that I would just not have the strength to bear it if the agony gathered in her broke free.

Chanthan was right. We ought to find a chieftain or a king, an arachan. We need a patron. We had heard that there were still ears in the great houses which yearned for the paanar's song.

Some of the young men supported him. He continued.

'We must rid ourselves of want and hardship. We must also find our friend, Mayilan. Did we not get to know that he lives in the land of the lord Nannan? We must go meet him. He must be there. Shouldn't we seek him out?'

No one had any objection.

'Let us set out tomorrow, without delay. Else no one here will stay alive for long. Let us talk to Perumpaanan.'

Everyone agreed.

When I returned home that evening, empty-handed as usual, Nellakkili said, 'Spare a thought at least for these helpless puppies. Cheera, too, has had nothing to eat.'

Cheera was sitting on the floor, still as a statue, her eyes fixed on the tiny bodies of the pups. They were drained of life except for the faint beating of their hearts. Chithira was scolding her.

That night I did not sleep. Nor did Nellakkili. Who knew better than us that when the body burned, so would its inner worlds? When we were ready to leave the next morning, all that was left to gather were our yaazhs and the paras – our music.

As we walked, Cheera kept turning back, as though she could hear the un-dead whimpers of the dead puppies. She must have seen them in every little patch of the ground in front of us, pushing their little bodies into the spaces between our legs, as though seeking the warmth of their mother's body.

The scent of akil spread from the forests by the wayside. The children stopped in their tracks gaping at the sight of the black female langurs swinging in the branches of the trees. Their mothers pulled them away by their arms. Some turned their eyes towards the hives around which the bees swarmed in large numbers. Some of the male monkeys eyed the bundles on our shoulders and stiffened their tails.

'What is this, Anna?'

Cheera's eyes widened, seeing people standing around a structure made of branches and ropes.

Ulakan heard her, but did not reply. He probably did not know what it was. Those were traps for wild boar set by the kuravar. The traps were still there because the prey had not fallen into them yet. The kuravar were dismantling them. Some of them had gone deep into the forest in pursuit of the elephants which had trampled on their crops. Seeing the approaching group of wayfarers, they asked us where we were bound. Perumpaanan answered them.

'Come to our huts,' they said. 'We have deer flesh and monitor lizard meat. Also bamboo seeds cooked in milk. Good for the children!'

We said no politely, but they would not hear of it. Still, we did not stay long in the kurava huts. The children ate the milk porridge. Rice cooked with deer flesh was packed in palm-leaf packets for our journey ahead. After the meal was over, they wanted us to perform the kuravakkoothu, but we did not have the time for it. On our way out, Cheera held out her hand to pluck some three-eyed leaves of the koovalam tree.

'Don't touch it, child! The eyes of the sky god will flash red! There will be a shower of fire!'

Cheera pulled back her hand abruptly. She always had a keen ear for anything to do with the inhabitants of the world beyond. Kottavai, Pavai of Kollimala, Kannagi of Koodal – they were the queens of her inner-worlds. You only had to say their names to make her obey.

The kanthal and kurinjhi were not in bloom, but they seemed to harbour the memory of springtime. We kept walking. Below us were clumps of bamboo in which birds frolicked. A large stream leapt out of the hill's topknot and vanished somewhere in between. We could see a small shrine beside the stream, perched like an eagle on the hill. We held our lutes and drums close so that they would be silent. People were coming down the hill. Some of them were umanar who were travelling to the next town to sell salt. Their women looked exhausted from holding their children with one hand and a whip in the other to drive their bullock-cart wagons. They stopped the carts by the wayside, held their children to their bosoms, leaned back and dozed. The bullocks shook their horns. They could smell the grass that pressed down on the rocks on the hillside.

We could see behind us the path which wound down the hill. Though we had walked a long way downhill, the feeling that we were still high above the ground lingered. The path we faced seemed to run upwards. The heights we had to scale left us dispirited. We sat down for a while and fed the children the meat and rice. The leftovers, we ate. When Ulakan collected the empty palm-leaf packets and was about to throw them away, Chanthan stopped him.

'Don't throw those away. Let us make rain-hats.'

Ulakan and Chanthan made rain-hats for the little ones, who now began to pine for rain.

The path became more and more quiet and deserted. We kept walking. Our heartbeats were like those of ants climbing a large heap of sand; our lives resembled their fleeting existence. My foot slipped. I grabbed a rock nearby for balance, but still tottered a bit. The path running upwards seemed quite slippery. I may lose my balance again, I thought. I gripped the rocks on the side and walked carefully. The rock faces were steep. And slippery. I moved ahead slowly, hands and feet slipping and staggering. In between, my fingers slid into a fissure in a rock. It felt slimy in there too. Moss, I thought – but sensing movement, I pulled my hand away instantly.

In a flash, a snake uncoiled! Hood swaying, it hissed at me once. I lurched, then fell down. The snake slid down the path quickly. For a second, everyone was motionless, and then they all screamed involuntarily. Unable to hurry on a path so narrow and slippery, they clung to each other, trembling.

24

The snake disappeared into the grass below the path swiftly. I was still panting, unable to pull myself up. I had sunk into the paste-like mud, which was now spread all over. When I stretched out my arm, some others who were holding on to the rocks with one hand held out their other hand to me. One of them managed to grab my hand. I gripped his slippery hand hard and raised myself up. There could be danger both ahead and behind. We were wilting with fear as we started to walk again, trembling and reluctant. Two little ones who were still fearful kept bawling. After a little while, dense forests appeared on either side of the path. The slightest stirring brought to our minds the spectre of a tiger, leopard or elephant. At every step we feared the slithering, twisting snakes raising their hoods at us.

'Someone climb a tree, look around, and call out what they see.' Hearing Perumpaanan's order, Chanthan smartly clambered up one. The trunks of the massive trees were slimy and hard to climb; so when those who climbed them halfway shouted that nothing was to be seen, they did not sound too sure. The viralis offered vows and offerings to Koothandavar. Others raised their hands towards the skies and began to weep and pray, first softly, and later, loudly.

Darkness began to fall. We held hands as we walked. The children hung on to their parents' fingers, keeping close to their bodies. Where the path dropped steeply, they sat and slid down the incline. Our fear was beginning to abate. We were moving ahead slowly when, suddenly, something bore swiftly into Ulakan's bundle. A bellow like a wounded cow collapsing on the ground rent the air! I started violently. Ulakan, who had let out a sharp yell, crashed down on the path. I bounded towards him. Lifting him up, I laid him on my lap and ran my hands over him. There were no wounds. He was terror-struck. I opened his bundle and felt inside. The leather surface of a pathalappara was torn. There was an arrow in it.

Seeing it, Perumpaanan quickly cried out aloud: 'We are wayfarers. Paanar and koothar. Please spare us!'

I turned to those who were with me, 'Take out your drums and beat them!'

The trees first, and then the undergrowth, began to stir.

'Don't be afraid!'

Men wearing quivers and carrying bows began to emerge from the wild. Some of them carried burning sticks of firewood.

They were kuravar who were guarding their millet fields from atop tree houses. They were watching out for elephants which destroyed the crop. The arrows were also meant for wild boar, if they ventured close. They had heard something stirring and thought that prey was approaching. That was why an arrow was shot.

26

'Where are you going in this dark?'

Perumpaanan told them. His voice quivered with emotion when he mentioned the places of rest that the aiynar and kuravar had lovingly offered us.

'You cannot go down this path in the dark. A little way downhill is the Aazhi river that brims over in the monsoon. There are fearsome crocodiles in it, the type which will not spare even massive elephants! You will see large rocks laid across the river and logs of wood that connect them. You have to step on those to cross the waters. You have to hold on to each other while crossing.

'Our huts are far away. It is quite a bit of a walk to get there. No one can go through the forest in the night. So we stay in our tree houses till daybreak. But if you can walk a little more, below the hill, there are rock caves in which people can rest. Stay there tonight and resume your journey in the morning.

'Be careful – if you slip on this path that runs down from here, you will lose your life! Hold on to the bamboo on either side when you walk, take care!'

We were about to bid goodbye to the kuravar when one of them arrived there with a captured boar, wounded and thrashing.

'This is for you. You can make a fire where you camp and cook this for supper!'

He cut the boar into pieces. The pulse of life seemed reluctant to leave its body. We were numb with hunger, beyond any courtesy. We plucked leaves from the trees, wrapped the meat pieces in them and added them to our bundles. The kuravar also lit a stick of firewood and handed it to us.

One of them came with us to show the way. He showed us how to stretch our arms and grasp the bamboos that stood at intervals on either side. We did as told. When we reached a stream in which waters from the mountains gushed, our guide stopped.

A large broken length of bamboo lay in front of us. One of the koothar held out the burning light towards it. We saw a body with many segments, with grey and yellow markings! The kuravan started back.

'Not bamboo, this is a python!'

We were petrified with fear once again. The python lay glinting like a huge smouldering tree in the waters that were reddish in the light of the fire. Not knowing how to cross, we retreated. The children hid behind our backs.

We stood there for a while. I had moved several steps back without realizing it. Rain began to fall again. Holding our lutes and drums in our laps, we sat down with bent backs. We were not able to keep our fire going because of the rain, but before the last leap of light, we saw something that left us astonished. The python glided downstream making a slippery-sounding noise, pushed down by an enormous current of water that came roaring from high above the hill.

The rain abated. We kept moving slowly, unable to see anything at all in the murky darkness, hitting something now, blocked by something else now, like a raft adrift. A little ahead, in the feeble light that appeared as the trees parted, we saw some open spaces.

'Isn't that light that we see ahead?' I asked aloud.

'Rock caves,' said the kuravan, our guide. 'Since people can't go any further at night, they stay there till the morning. You can stay there too.'

Before long, we reached the place where the light was. These were caves carved out of the rock at the bottom of the hill – its crevasses widened into habitable spaces. Someone was staying in one.

'We are wayfarers – paanar and koothar. May we have some fire, please?'

A man came out with a burning piece of firewood. He lit ours with it and went back. 'You will be fine,' he did not forget to tell us, as we stood before him brimming with silent thanks, our palms folded in respect. We lowered our bundles in the unoccupied caves. The children's bellies were burning – that we could see without their telling us anything. We built a fire in the open space in front of the caves and started roasting the wild boar.

We watched hungrily as the pieces of boar, red and inviting, were being roasted. So intent were we that we did not hear our neighbour, the occupant of the next cave, approach. Only when we heard something shift did we turn around and see him. Ah, is this the Divine

Aandavan in flesh and blood? I could not help asking myself. The lotus flower in his hair had not yet wilted. The silk waistcloth that he wore shone in the firelight.

'You are still in great need, aren't you?' He asked with a hint of a smile on his lips.

Perumpaanan's cheeks stiffened. It was shameful to reveal one's want to another.

'Do not be ashamed. I am a paanan too, like you. I too was poor. But no longer. I praised some rulers in song. They gave me more than I need.'

After a moment's reluctance, Perumpaanan asked him: 'May we know your name?'

'Paranar.'

'Ah! Perumpulavare! Salutations to you, Great Master of Song!' Those were the words that escaped our Perumpaanan as his body pulsed in immense elation. He bowed his head in deep respect. The lines of a palai song that Paranar had written came to my lips. It was one that Nellakkili sang all the time.

From tender mango buds
The colour has faded,
Their rising beauty has fallen.
Like the pichaka flower in the grass
Her brow is now so pale, so jaded.
Her lovely eyes, like a picture drawn,
Eyes that flow like the rain,
They well in the pain of parting.

Paranar's eyes grew wide. Then they shone with tears.

Three

Meeting the Perumpulavar made us forget everything. For a brief while, we even forgot that our children's bellies burned with hunger. Seeing the celebrated Paranar up close, we were overcome with joy. This paanan, who had learned all that he learned through song – what made his eyes fill with tears? We were curious to know. I asked him the question.

'My friends, that was the song I wrote in the memory of Aathimanthi, the daughter of Karikala Chozhan who built the grand anicut on the Kaveri.'

The great songster moved closer to the fire and sat down. We pricked up our ears. The light that sprouted from the eyes of the listeners threw its tendrils into the valleys of their eyes and then spread towards their cheeks.

'Aathimanthi the Wise. Accomplished in dance and music. Beautiful.'

Paranar paused for a moment and pointed to Chithira: 'Look, like this one.'

Chithira lowered her face coyly.

Smiling, Paranar continued. 'Her husband was Atthi, of the Vanchinaad king's clan. Because he was a skilled dancer, he was called Aattanatthi. Unmatched in physical prowess and dance. He was . . . like . . . this young chap!'

He meant Chanthan. I scratched my head.

'They dwelt on the banks of the Kaveri, and were lost in song and dance. From their entwined fingers bloomed thick-petalled blossoms. Simmering dragonflies rose from their eyes. Body on body, they sculpted beauty to rhythm and music; it made even the Kaveri playful.'

Chanthan sent a furtive glance towards Chithira. She did not return it. Good. She was absorbed in the story, her ears alert.

'When the Kaveri waved to them with her ever-prancing hands, they went to her. Their joyful play continued in the waters of the river. Suddenly, the current swelled. Aattanatthi was swept away. Kaveri drew him into her whirlpools in an ever-tightening embrace. He struggled with its depths and the forceful torrents below. Seeing that her husband was missing, Aathimanthi looked again and again pleadingly at the Kaveri and wept. She had somehow scrambled back onto the riverbank and now wandered there, distraught and afraid. Overcome by sorrow, she stumbled and fell at each step.'

Paranar paused to clear his throat.

'And then . . .?'

Cheera's eyes had widened. She drew back her hand that had been pressed down on the floor and held it to her chin.

'I will tell you, child! A woman had been bathing in the next ghat – Maruthi. She ran towards Aathimanthi and held her. She could see Aattanatthi being carried away by the swift waters to the sea. She pointed towards the current flowing to the sea. They ran to the beach. There, far away on the waves of the sea, was Aattanatthi, now bobbing, now sinking. Seeing the sea take him, Aathimanthi sank down in despair. Maruthi rushed towards the sea and leapt in. Soon, she disappeared among the waves.

'Standing on the beach, Aathimanthi called out: "Alas, my man with chiselled, broad shoulders, where are you?"

'She awaited a reply from the surging waters. The rolling sounds of the sea pushed down all the answers her call may have brought forth. Suddenly, she noticed two forms bobbing up and down on the crest of the waves. When one of them was washed closer, she ran into the sea. She grabbed Aattanatthi's body, which the waves brought towards the shore, and dragged him onto the beach. Hugging him as close as she could, Aathimanthi broke into piteous sobs. She called out his name again and again, shaking him by his shoulders.

'"Awake, my hero, my broad-shouldered one!"

'Her tears fell on his eyes and cheeks and flowed down his body through the skin's pathways. He opened his eyes.'

'He lifted his trembling fingers and touched the extravagant flood of her beautiful tresses. Looking into her reddened, rain-filled eyes, he said, "Oh, merciful woman, the sea itself returned me to you seeing your firmness and great love!"

'"No! It is Maruthi who returned you to me, my lord! Ayyo! Where is she?"'

'Ayyo! Where is she?' asked Cheera, who was all ears. Her question sounded louder than she meant it to be.

'The sea took Maruthi instead of Aattanatthi.'

Paranar's voice trailed off. Filled with the thought of the woman gone rather than the man who was returned, Cheera was quiet, her head bowed.

'Perumpulavare, is there a song about her?'

A great sorrow began to seep into all of us too. Paranar did not speak. All our dear ones who had passed began to gather within our hearts unsummoned. When even the breeze hung heavy, our Perumpaanan asked: 'Let that be! Master, how did you come to be here?'

'Don't you know this place?' He asked in return. 'This is Umberkaadu. Don't you hear the resonant hum of the Aazhi? I sang the praises of the Chera king Velkezhukuttuvan. You must have heard too? He is the conqueror of Kodukoor. He defeated Pazhayan and cut down his sacred neem tree! He is the Chenguttuvan who rolled back the sea! My song filled his mind with light! Pleased, he bestowed on me all the wealth that Umberkaadu produces.'

'Yes, we have heard of him. He who cut off the locks of the women of the defeated and turned them into braids to tether the elephants . . .' Chanthan repeated what he had heard somewhere.

That seemed to vex Paranar. His look, as sharp as a spearhead, flew towards Chanthan. He rose quickly from where he sat and strode away.

'Perumpulavare, please forgive him if he has spoken evil,' begged our Perumpaanan, folding his palms respectfully and throwing a dagger of a look at Chanthan.

Paranar did not stop. He went into his cave.

A dark shadow fell upon all of us songmakers. Perumpaanan sat with his head bent low.

After a short while, a light appeared at the door of the rock cave. When Paranar approached him, Perumpaanan stood up.

'All hearsay is not the truth. I have never been able to know the truth about rulers. But there is one thing that I know: the paanar and koothar need a way out of lack. The king needs praise, and poets to sing those praises. What else do we have to escape our poverty but song and dance?'

Chanthan cleared his throat. He glanced at Perumpaanan and then withdrew.

Paranar carried on: 'I can hear this question ring inside you: who will speak up to a ruler when he is a wrongdoer? The same question turns inside me too, like a turnstile, each time I compose a song.'

'Let that be,' he said. 'You must eat something. The children must be famished.'

We remembered food only then. Some had fallen asleep, drained by hunger. As we shared the roasted meat, Paranar asked, 'Where are you going?'

'As you noted, your honour, we are tormented by lack and hunger. It is said that the ruler of Ezhimala, Nannan, is a lover of dance and music. We are on our way to see him.'

My reply seemed to leave him speechless for a few moments. Then, in a low voice, he asked, 'Nannan? You are going to see him? What do you know of him?'

'We have heard a little. You yourself have sung about him – the chieftain who defied the Great Three!'

'Yes. But that Nannan exists no more. He lost the battle with the Chera king and went into hiding. He was killed, I hear.'

I felt weak – left with no strength to even glance at Nellakkili. Where were we to seek Mayilan now? Would it be possible to at least find out if he was still alive?

'Are you not paanar and koothar? For the paanan to thrive, he must know the land. He must know the ruler of the land. You, however, have not even heard of the terrible killings from years ago! The Nannan of today is the son of the Nannan of the past. He is the ruler of the land known as Chenganma, on the banks of the Cheyyaar. The famed city that today's Nannan rules is at the foot of Navira Hill. But this road will not take you there.'

Perumpaanan looked stunned with surprise.

'We know nothing of rulers, pulavare. It is said that our ancestors migrated from Kuttanaad. They had accompanied the Chera king when he moved to Vanchi, singing his praises and dancing for him. We settled down in a small area on the sides of the great mountain he conquered, the Aanamala. But then the rulers took to new songsters, and the lineages of the older singers became worthless! Still, we sang and danced in lands near our dwelling place. We go to houses, alone or in groups, and fix the payment. Then, after the night of music and dance, we take what they give us and leave. The homes of the uzhavar and chantor always have abundant food and drink. But such folk are rare in that area. There are almost no stately homes and fields yielding abundant harvests. We have heard of some rulers through songs; from some of your songs too. We also sing them when we dance. Beyond that, we know nothing about the kings of distant lands. We were bound for Ezhimala. We had heard that Nannan reigns there . . .'

Our Perumpaanan sounded very worried.

'Yes. The elder Nannan reigned in Ezhimala. He was renowned for many feats. You must have known too, through the songs. His defeat of the Chera at Pazhi . . .'

'What happened to him?' I asked.

'He could not hold against the powerful Chera,' said Paranar. 'Narmudicheral's army defeated him. He escaped and took refuge in the eastern hills. But the Chera army cornered and defeated him at Vaakapperumthurai. Nannan died fighting . . .'

It seemed that Paranar could not stop speaking of this ruler he knew so well. But fathomless grief pervaded his eyes.

'Perumpulavare,' I addressed him. 'There is another reason why we have set out for Ezhimala. My son . . . he went away from home at a very young age. A traveller told us that he had seen him at Ezhimala. We seek him.'

'In Ezhimala? I was there for a long while. What is his name?'

'I don't know if you'll know the name. Your honour, it is Mayilan. My eldest boy.'

'Mayilan?' Shock and sorrow rang together in Paranar's voice.

'Yes. He left young. Since then, we have heard nothing from him.'

Paranar seemed drained of words for a few moments. 'I know a Mayilan, born in a paana home.'

'You know him? Oh, master! Where is he now?'

The Perumpulavar seemed to be struggling. It was as though he was trying to quell a great clang within.

'You seem to want to say something, master. Please speak!'

'No. I had to leave Ezhimala. I have heard nothing about him since I left. I have nothing to say.'

'He's been missing since he was a boy. Please, his loved ones are all here, trying to find him. Please have mercy on us. Please tell us whatever you know.'

'Did I not tell you? I knew him well. But I have heard nothing of him since I left the place. All I can say for sure is that he is alive.'

His words were firm; they stopped us from probing any further. We held our tongues.

'Did you not see a shrine on the way here?' he asked us.

'Yes. We passed it. We did not visit it.'

'You should have gone there. Maybe you met me for just that! You can also reach it if you climb up by this side of the hill. It is late now. Sleep well. Tomorrow, make sure that you go there before you leave. In fact, decide where to go after you visit the shrine.'

Paranar's advice made us look at each other. The confusion about where to go and what to do was evident on each of our faces.

Though the downpour had subsided, the waters flowing down from the top of Aanamala continued to rage. Below, the Aazhi river must be in full spate.

The resonant wail of a waterfall – that fell hard on the rocks before it became a river – turned into a roar that sounded louder still in the silence of the night. I lay down on the floor of the rock cave, eyes closed but unable to sleep. The waterfall's crashing and rumbling seemed to be rising up from my heart.

Four

Even when I dozed off fleetingly in the middle of that sleepless night, nightmares shook me awake. The sharp points that gleamed in Paranar's words when he mentioned Mayilan had grown into a huge thicket of thorns – they now hung heavy on my eyelashes. Mayilan is in some trouble or the other. He has hurt Paranar. The master will not speak of it. I could gauge little of it – except that I started violently awake, hearing in my dream the last heart-rending screams from a battle thick with shadows and bloodied bodies. The others had not slept either. Everyone woke early. No one knew where to go, which lord to approach. Like me, they too must have thought – better to follow Paranar's advice; perhaps he told us to visit the shrine so that we would know our destination.

We did not have to walk much to reach it. Only during the climb did we realize how little we had moved from where we were on the slippery path. The jungle grew dense as we went up the slope which led to the shrine. Wild gooseberry and karimaruthu trees grew profusely. The scents of flowers and fruits unknown to us spread there. Do not tarry taking them in, said Paranar, hurrying us on. Seeing the frolicsome monkeys swinging in the trees on which the bees had built their hives, the children stopped. No, don't stop at the sight, Paranar insisted.

The master songster must have feared that the allurements of the wild might mislead us. The pieces of ripe jackfruit that slipped from the fingers of the monkeys gave out a mesmerizingly honeyed scent. It aroused the children's cravings, but the adults pulled them along firmly as they walked quickly. The mist that rose from the smaller streams tumbling on the rocks soon wrapped itself around us. The sound of water falling haplessly sounded like a scream. The children struggled to scramble up the steep path. But probably because it was early in the morning, we were not exhausted. We reached the foot of a banyan tree on which birds of many colours chirped. The shrine was near, it seemed.

The holy place we had seen from afar the day before now appeared closer in sight. On all four sides, the burgeoning forest. In the middle, a placid little shrine. Many kinds of mango trees were in bloom in its front yard. It began to drizzle as we drew near. The peacocks were dancing there, their open plumes shiny with raindrops. We went past them into the shrine. Besides us, there were just a couple of others.

'The rain here will not stop, ever. Such is the sadness of she who dwells within. It will always brim over and rain down.'

We looked at each other, unable to grasp what Paranar meant. He pointed to the inner sanctum, joining his palms together respectfully.

I too folded my hands and turned towards the sanctum. The sight was staggering.

Inside the sanctum in which no lamps shone was a stone doll. It looked like a little girl sleeping with her eyes open – or lying dead. The doll was covered with a piece of red cloth. I suddenly felt that we were in the middle of a cremation. Unable to pray, I looked at Paranar.

'This little girl was murdered by Nannan.'

Paranar's lips trembled. Perhaps there was a shrillness to his voice, for one of the worshippers turned to look at us.

'Ah! No matter who they are – near and dear, or those from afar – there is no difference in how they treat women! Drown the fallen land in slaughter. Burn the crops. Chop off the tear-drenched locks of the widowed women. Is that not the custom of the powerful?'

That was Chithira. She had just said aloud things that she had learned from songs.

'No, friends, this is different. I told you earlier, I have not been able to discern the good and the bad of rulers. But it is not possible to forgive Nannan's terrible crime against one who had not yet outgrown child's play. The murder of women is not our custom. It should never be.'

Chithira and Cheera were now listening keenly.

'I have sung of her many times.'

Even Perumpaanan's furrowed brows rose in anticipation. I realized with a shudder that she, the deity, though invisible, now filled the air around us. She was staring at us with smouldering eyes, her hair in wild disarray. Paranar began to speak, his voice rasping.

'Nannan had a prized mango grove. Many rare types of mango trees, brought from distant parts, grew in it. A truly tempting scent would rise from the ripening mangoes during the mango season. Children and adults would gaze at those bunches with deep longing. But the grove was guarded well. Armed men patrolled, constantly watching the place with sharp eyes. Anyone stealing a single mango from the orchard would surely die. And even if a single mango was stolen, the guards would die – that was the price of negligence. All knew that the ruler was one whose word was inflexible. The fear of death is common to all; no one showed the pluck to defy his decree.

'Ah, but what was one to do? The heavy axe of the law fell on a little girl who in her innocence knew neither the custom nor her ruler's severity. She had been playing in the waters of the Aazhi river with her friends when a ripe mango floated by. Not knowing that the fruit was forbidden to her, she ate it. Nannan ordered her to be killed. Her loved ones wept helplessly and begged for mercy. He did not relent. Rulers who err must be held back by those who stay by their side. They too looked away. And so she was killed. That little girl now remains in a state of sleepless slumber in this shrine. The mango tree which was Nannan's sacred tree began to die slowly after. Its boughs broke many times after that fateful day.'

Cheera and Chithira stood rooted to the spot, quivering. I could not bring myself to take a second look at the idol.

We stepped out, and then noticed something that had slipped our eye on our way in. This was a structure built on a block of stone in the temple courtyard. The man who had glanced at us while we were praying in the temple was rubbing a reddish spice paste on it. Washed down by the rain, the paste had spread on the earth all around.

Before we could ask what this was about, Paranar said, 'This is the Stone of Justice. See the red that spreads around it like blood? That red will never fade. People here say that those who rub the stone with spice paste will receive justice. I have always found the colour of blood that bubbles on this stone and its pungent heat searing. Nannan, who sacrificed mercy to blind justice, must be wandering here somewhere too . . . dead but without the peace of death. I know that.'

We heard the man rubbing the paste on the stone mumble something; we turned to him. He fell silent, but his eyes overflowed.

Paranar noticed it.

'Who are you?' he asked. 'Why do you weep?'

He did not speak. Instead, his eyes wandered from the door of the sanctum to the Stone of Justice and back again.

I went up to him and held him gently by his shoulders.

'My friend, are not sorrows the fate of all beings? Do not weep. You need not speak if you are loath to.'

'No,' he replied. 'It is not hesitation. I choked on my words.'

He wiped his tears. We were about to leave when he called out to us. 'Wait, let me tell you.'

We stopped.

'I don't know why I am telling you this,' he began. 'It is no use telling it to anyone.

'My woman and I lived in a village close by here. We were inseparable. Soon, her womb bore fruit. She could not live without me.'

His voice broke.

'I begged her many times to stay with her mother during the pregnancy. She would not listen. By the time she told me that we should get to the midwife who lived near Amma's house, her water had broken! It was very late. We started out for the midwife's house, though she was in no condition to walk. The night was so dark, it was impossible to find our way. The forest, so dense! She was exhausted, and I too grew weary as the path seemed to grow more and more unfamiliar. In the end, she could not even walk. Leave me under this tree, find the midwife and bring her here, she told me. I could not leave her there alone, so I lingered, but her heart-rending cries made me leave and seek the midwife. Groping through the blinding darkness, I reached the midwife's house. I knocked; when she opened the door, I blurted out why I was there. She shuddered. I could not see why, at that moment. Calling the village headman and two neighbours to come along, she hurried back with me. When we reached the place where my woman lay . . . the sight! I cannot speak of it even now, my friends!'

For a few moments, he was unable to talk.

'She was dead. So also the newborn infant. The blood still seeped into the ground and spread everywhere. I thought that my living spirit had shot out of my body splitting it in two. Someone held me as I collapsed. When I came to again, that midwife was sitting beside me. She was panting and sobbing, not knowing what to tell me. Then she told me why she had started so on seeing me. Early that dawn, she had a terrifying dream. That a woman thrashing about in childbirth was waiting for her in the impermeable darkness of the deep forest! In her dream, she set out there, but a ghoul lay in wait to attack her. She pushed it away and escaped, but as she ran, she was knocked down by a cow that suddenly appeared. The ghoul cornered her and grabbed her arm. She screamed out aloud and fought it with all her might. Suddenly, the murky skies were rent apart and shattered by an immense bolt of lightning! She felt instantly energized. That strength made her overcome the monster and kill it.'

What was the meaning of this nightmare? We were keen to know.

'She interpreted it for me,' he said. 'The strength that filled her, it came from the deity of this temple. Her dream revealed that the deity of this shrine was reborn in my woman's belly . . . to rid the world of that ghoul which had ruthlessly preyed on women.'

An innocent little girl, murdered by the king first, and then thwarted in rebirth . . .

He finished his story, pausing and stammering in between. No one uttered a word. All of us were probably examining our own sorrows quietly, measuring and weighing them.

Paranar said to him, 'Look, friend, I can see that the ample light of mercy that flows from this shrine is holding you close.'

Then he turned to us.

'She will be born again and again, differently each time. To be waylaid again and again by that warped thing that they call justice – the justice of the arachar, earthly kings, and aandavar, divine gods. It is not just mercy but also vengeance that stays undiminished in her. In the fullness of time she will shower on the world both mercy and reprisal . . .'

We could not tarry longer. The distraught husband and father still stood there. I took his hand in mine.

'Do not grieve, my friend. Why don't you come with us?'

'I cannot leave. She who was born to me is here. I want to see her every day. Till I can join her dead mother and her, I must at least live this life of togetherness.'

We could say nothing to him. As we left the place and stepped into the forest path behind Paranar, Cheera kept looking back.

'I am the deity of this shrine reborn,' she said. It must have sounded like a light-hearted remark to Chithira, who laughed.

Five

The energy and enthusiasm of earlier were missing during the descent. Why did Paranar take us up there? To convince us that we paanar and koothar should know what rulers are like? Or to persuade us that we needed to think about where justice for the powerful and for others joined and parted? Probably he, the master of song, intended all this. We were still floundering, unsure as to what to do or where to go. Paranar would show us the way, I felt. But he was silent about it; it worried me.

My thoughts were not wrong. When we neared the rock caves, he spoke: 'Now you have learned some things about how kings rule and how they act. Cruelty and compassion are twins born of the same womb. Separating the two in the act of ruling is difficult. Compassion towards one may be cruelty towards another. When you make songs about the powerful, remember this. Then you will see why you were taken to that shrine. May the sacred idol shower mercy on you!'

After a brief pause, he continued. 'Ah, let it be! Now, which lord are you going to see?'

'You must tell us whom to meet, master. We had planned to go to Ezhimala. This hunger and want must end. We must find Mayilan.'

'I do not know how the place is now. Mayilan, you will surely meet somewhere. I feel that you must not go to Ezhimala.'

We did not say anything. A throbbing pain within me left me wordless.

Paranar too seemed lost in thought. Then he said, 'There is a Vel named Paari in Parambumala. He is known for his munificence – so much so that he is called Vellal. He is fascinated by music and dance. He will heal your hardship.'

'But, master, we know nothing about him . . .' Perumpaanan said in a low whisper.

'Do not worry about that. Paari is strong, but his heart yields easily. His valour and arms are such that even the Great Three together cannot defeat him. He is felled only by music and dance! Kapilar, our common friend, lives there. He has sung much of Paari. Go, meet him. He will help you get an audience with Paari.'

'Yes, master, we will.' Perumpaanan must have felt that this was the best course to take.

'Make your way towards Parambumala. It is not far from here, and the road is not hard to find. May good things happen to you!'

We felt that Paranar's mind was drifting off. He probably planned to go elsewhere. We decided to part ways with him.

'Master, we have nothing to offer in return for your kindness. We therefore keep our gratitude to you safe in our hearts. May the gods be ever merciful to you!'

Paranar smiled as Perumpaanan said this.

'Play the Kurinjhippann for the hill gods! Did you not come this far safe?'

No sooner had these words fallen from his lips than Perumpaanan turned to look at me. Before he had called out my name, I had the periyaazh ready. Mallika sang in Perumpaanan's hands. The humming of the Aazhi river dissolved in her melody. We saluted the hills with deep bows.

It did not seem that Paranar was in a hurry to leave; so we saluted him with joined palms and prepared to leave first. As we walked on, I turned my head to look at him one last time. Paranar had vanished. Maybe he was inside the rock cave. Or maybe he had forgotten the world and immersed himself in his own song about friendship.

Before long, we reached the banks of the Aazhi. As the kuravar had said, there were large boulders in the river that led to the opposite bank. Probably because the rains had not advanced much, the logs connecting them had not been dislodged by the currents or submerged in them. But the flowing waters stroked and poked at the logs and even fought with them in some places.

We clambered one by one onto the single-log bridge that connected the banks with the boulders. Parts of the log were quite slimy. The bigger children sat on the log and shuffled ahead carefully on their buttocks. The senior folk placed their bundles in front of them and moved them, pushing forward slowly. Cheera held my hand tight. We reached the first boulder and waited for the others to catch up. Chanthan had held Chithira by her hand to help her walk on the log.

She must have told him that she could do it on her own; so he had left her side and was now helping Nellakkili who came up behind them. I found myself valuing him even more, though the sight of him made me melt from within, like wax in a flame. Where were we to now seek Mayilan?

Though the river was in spate, the waters were lucid. The sludge flowing down from the swamps on its banks could not muddy it. Sunshine wobbled and tottered on the watery expanse of the river, like the eyes of a newborn babe taking in the world. Then a shaft of lightning pierced the water and reached right down to its bottom; for a moment, the river sparkled like a crystal basin.

Seeing the trees that stood on the riverbanks stand on their heads in the water, Cheera let out a low giggle.

'Acha, will newborn babes also see the world like this, upside down? Who'd be seeing it right side up? Them or us?'

She tried to walk a few steps on her own. Her leg slipped a little and she lost her balance; it made even her ringing voice jar a bit.

She had been rummaging around in her thoughts since we had set out again in the morning. It seemed that she was looking for a lot more, now that we had reached the riverbank and were crossing the river, cutting across its light.

'Inside the newborn is a clear sky,' I told her. 'And then its hue changes. Sometimes it looks white. Sometimes blue. Then red. Or black.'

I knew her inner world, and so I crafted a reply that spoke to it.

'Why does the colour of the sky change all the time?'

'The sky is colourless, my daughter! It fools our eyes. Like the sky, this whole world too is a lie, some say.'

I was not sure if I should tell her about the many-hued coverlets that we weave to cloak the emptiness of this world and delude the eyes. Or maybe, emptiness does not exist either. There must exist in the world something to see, to hear, to know by touch. But don't we weave the warm covers of dreams and memories over our dearth of this and that? What do newborn babies dream of when they begin to see the world?

'Now the sky is white,' began Cheera again, seeing the flocks of vellari cranes rise into the sky.

'Where are they flying to?'

'To the fields nearby, maybe.'

'We are like these birds. Right, Acha?'

I frowned.

'From the riverbank to the fields; from one land to another. Neither the land we came from, nor the land we come into, are ours to rest and take root. The birds have no land of their own, am I not right, Acha?'

Her manner of perceiving and grasping each little thing amazed me; it also left me a little afraid.

'Yes, my dear. No one has a place that they can call their own forever. Our dear ones are always near us; but then everyone is dear to us. Did you not see how the aiynar and the kuravar and the master treated us? The goodness and the badness we talk of do not arise because someone else acts in some way. Joy and sorrow are not given to us by another. Life and death have been eternally in this world since it was born. Do you see these logs on which we now cross this river? They move with the river's currents, don't they? They are always trying to free themselves and follow the tide! Just like that, something is taking us from one place to another. These are things that the wise ones of long ago have already said. Maybe we write our lives as we fly through the inner recesses of the wind, like birds, with our wings.'

'We write in our emptiness, don't we? No one reads that, Acha.'

She already knew of life that turns into barren waste! Not knowing whether to be proud or to weep, I kissed her on the head. Cheera saw how even in the fullness of sunshine, the trees on the opposite bank had turned into the curving kavadi poles of green and black. Legs will shoot out of the roots of one of those trees and rush here, cutting through the ripples, she imagined. Jolted, she withdrew her gaze. Like someone who had been woken from a dream but simply could not recall what it was that woke them up. She held the edge of a moss-covered rock and the fringe of her skirt tightly and sat down, shutting her eyes. I noticed a circle of light around her. The deity of the shrine, the little girl who slept on her funeral pyre, had come down to her, I felt. She was holding Cheera in her lap and caressing her.

Though the kuravar had warned us about crocodiles, we saw none. But each of us saw in our inner eye one of their kind crouch silently on a mud-covered boulder like frozen bloodthirst. They could gobble down anything – from fish to an elephant. Tales of crocodiles devouring their own young made us shudder. Keep us from encountering such a beast, we kept praying to the gods till we reached the other bank. Fear held us by a tight rope until each of us got to the other side safe, crawling on the logs and slipping on the boulders. Our trembling bodies soon began to relax, seeing women on the other side leaving the bathing ghats clad in fresh clothes and decked with alluring blue peacock feathers. But even after we had made the crossing, some among us found it hard to speak.

The sights from up close were quite different from what they appeared to be from a distance. Solitary mango trees laden with fruit stood tall here and there on heaps of silt by the riverside. The reeds grew skyward, reaching above the thickets, swaying in the wind. Their white flowers are like cranes, said Cheera, smiling.

We walked on. Most of us had cheered up now that our fear had abated. Where were Nellakkili and Chithira? I turned around to look. They were right behind. Ulakan? He was not anywhere near. Must be taking his time, chatting with the other children. But he was not with them. I went back in search of him, to quite some distance. There they stood, Ulakan and Chanthan, in a thicket beside the river. They were discussing something.

'What are you doing here?' I asked in a rather harsh tone.

Ulakan did not answer.

'Where will we seek Mayilan? If we cannot find him, no matter what gains we make, will we heal?'

Chanthan stood there with his head bowed, as if he had taken my despair on his head.

'Acha, we are leaving for Ezhimala to seek Annan.'

Chanthan grabbed Ulakan's wrist.

'No, you must go with your family. I have no debts of duty to repay now, do I? I will find him by myself, wherever he may be.'

When Chanthan said that, I was wrung by a dilemma.

'Do not leave, my child,' I told him. 'There will be a time to meet him someday. You need to just come with us.'

Though I said that, I did not know how we would find Mayilan. But I remembered Paranar's words. We would find him someday for sure.

Chanthan was adamant. I failed in the face of his youthful grit and vigour. I tried to persuade him against his decision even as we walked ahead. We did not have to walk for long. Our folk were waiting for us ahead.

At the sound of our footfall, herons rose up from the curving branches of the gangly marutha trees. Peacocks perched, ears alert, plumes folded, on the boughs of mango trees. A little ahead, vast paddy fields opened up on either side of the path. The uzhavar, who were busy weeding, saw us and stopped working. We too brightened inwardly seeing other people.

A man with a grey beard undid his headgear, gave it a good shake, and came up to us. Seeing the bundles of lutes and drums on our shoulders, he must have guessed our trade. Still, he raised a surprised brow as though it were customary to do so.

'Where are you bound for? We have not seen you here before.'

'We are bound for Parambumala,' our Perumpaanan told him. 'We seek to meet Vel Paari. We have heard of his generosity. That he gives his own land to even the beggars who go to him seeking land.'

'True,' the man replied. 'Vel Paari is a hero, but soft of heart. That serves beggars rather well! No need to work all day and night for a living, they may think.'

His words struck a sensitive spot.

'We are no beggars. We make our living from music and dance. If you are cattle, of course, you wouldn't need dance and song!'

It was Chanthan. The thorns in the man's words had drawn blood.

'We don't have the time to argue!' I got in the middle. 'Let's go, child!'

It was noon by then. The children were tired of walking. This did not look like a land that offered rest and warmth.

We kept walking. For those who are blessed with abundant wealth and fortune that the earth so benevolently bestows, the pain of others might look like a joke.

We passed by a large paddy field. The path we trod looked like the ridges of the field had just been flattened; it offered no shade. The hot noon wind cooled a little at the touch of the rice saplings that filled the fields. The sun blazed less by the time we crossed them. Now on either side there were kanchi trees in full bloom and mango trees with large bunches of mangoes hanging from them. We could spot the parrots on the boughs only when we peered carefully at the green. On the wayside ahead there were a couple of porters' stones and a water fountain. The children scampered towards the shade. The men lowered their bundles onto the porters' rests. The women hurried to draw water.

I saw Chanthan sitting under a mango tree, away from the group, his head bowed. I went towards him. He lifted his face towards me; he looked glum.

'What happened to you, child?'

He did not reply. After a few moments, he murmured as though in reply to me.

'We must be like woodworms? Parasites?'

My forehead crinkled.

'We are creatures that make hollows outside our bodies and let our living spirits roost there. That is where our dance and song are. Those who seek the living spirit inside their bodies have no need for spaces outside.'

'Chantha, haven't you dropped it yet? Aren't there different kinds of people? The uzhavar live by their labour. They value sweat. Let it go! All that I heard today can be made into song – Cheera thinks that we are birds; you think that we are woodworms!'

Ulakan and some other older children were up on the mango trees. The ones who were too little to climb stood below, holding out their hands and asking for some fruit. Ulakan and his friends plucked some ripe and near-ripe mangoes and dropped them into the waiting hands below. The children feasted on the mangoes and ran off for a sip of water. The older people followed them, seeking rest. They stretched out or sat in groups in the shade of the trees. I sat down under the mango tree; telling myself that this was a short rest, I closed my eyes.

The sound of a small crowd chattering woke me up. Some people were talking with our Perumpaanan; they were uzhavar. I went towards them with a few others.

'There is an annual festival at the uzhavar's temple that lasts for seven days. They ask if we could sing and dance there. Kolumba, what do you say?'

The uzhavar moved away and waited at a distance. Chanthan hurried to us.

'You think that it is all right to forget that insult so soon?' he rasped.

'A wound should be stitched together, not pulled apart,' said Perumpaanan, without raising his voice.

Chanthan did not challenge him, but it was evident that he did not agree.

'Singing and dancing are how we earn our bread. Some dealings may not be easy, but we must still perform.'

I could not contradict him.

'So, what are you going to say?'

'Ask for a good sum as payment. No need to make it cheap.'

Chanthan returned to the shade of the tree. I followed him. Perumpaanan must have spoken tactfully with the uzhavar and settled on a sum. We don't generally interfere when he deals with such matters. Perumpaanan gestured to us to follow the uzhavar. I took Chanthan's hand, urging him to come with us. He pulled his hand away gently.

'I am not coming. I am setting off for Ezhimala.'

Though I knew that even long hours of persuasion would not help, I made one last entreaty.

'What will become of us if you aren't there dancing?'

'Everything will be fine even without me. It will be a matter of shame for the koothar if they rely too much on one person.'

I said no more. My feet dragged, but I followed the others. Where was Chithira? I looked around. She was quite some way ahead, sharing a joke with Cheera and laughing.

I could not help turning back to look. Chanthan stood there motionless, his eyes still fixed on us. A whimper, which sounded like the ripping cry of a strand torn out of the stem of a coconut frond, rushed up my throat, but I pushed it down.

Six

Chanthan's unwavering gaze stayed with me as I followed the uzhavar. No one else knew of his decision. When I sensed a selfish sense of relief manifest within me at the thought that it was not Ulakan but Chanthan who was going in search of Mayilan, I cringed in shame.

'Chanthan is not coming with us,' I shouted, not aiming to reach any particular ear.

All except Ulakan stopped suddenly, taken aback. The fire inside me seared him too. Chithira covered her mouth, frowning. I told everyone what had happened. Some wanted to go and get him to come back. If he isn't coming, we aren't coming either — others said. But our wise Perumpaanan forbade them from approaching him.

'He will find good news and come back with it.'

I too felt that Perumpaanan's inner eye might be right. Though crestfallen, the rest of us went towards where the uzhavar took us.

The blooming evening flowers announced the arrival of dusk. The cattle that had gone to graze were returning home.

In the little ponds on the wayside, richly petalled blue and white lotuses rested on placid, azure waters. Reddish fish flitted among them. People cast nets to catch fish from the ponds; others used fishing rods. They were now returning home with their catch. A gentle breeze sprinkled coolness on our bodies.

The uzhavars' dwellings came into view. Many of these were large mansions, with long cowsheds and spacious granaries alongside. Their roofs were thatched with hay and the walls were plastered with cow dung. Some women were busy pouring the parboiled paddy left out to dry in the sun into large baskets. They shooed away the house sparrows that hopped up to peck at the grain. So absorbed were they in their labours that they did not notice us. The cows had returned from the grazing grounds to their sheds. The women who hurried there with milking pots threw us casual glances, but did not come up to meet us; they were probably in a hurry. But the girls playing near their houses, who wore the evening blooms in their hair, stared, seeing strangers in us. Some of them left their playthings. Play carts stopped rolling. Our bundles seemed to unsettle them; they did not come near.

Their garments shone! Their necklaces were of gold!

Cheera could not contain her awe. She was very fond of children and grew close to them quickly. But she held herself back from going towards these little ones. Of course, she had never seen such clothes and toys.

We stood around feeling diffident. Soon, the uzhavar who were with us led us to their houses. Ulakan and I and some others were to be lodged at the house of an uzhavan named Azhakan. Cheera went with her mother to another house. Some of our women went with them.

The dusk began to deepen. The sounds of women de-husking paddy with pestles of ivory on stone mortars lingered in the air. I rested my tired eyes for a little while, listening to the vella song that they sang. A woman sang her ire about her husband who had spent the night at the house of some harlot of a paraththa, dancing the thunanga koothu with her. He was back in the morning, fresh after a bath. Of what use, feminine virtues? Good birth? When your husband comes back from cavorting all over the breasts of pleasure girls and their welcoming honeypots, with their teeth marks on his shoulders, you must greet him brightly, without a trace of protest! If not, he will seek them even more!

'Are you asleep?'

It was Azhakan.

'If you are rested from the journey, we could go to the temple. With the others, too.'

I got up. All of us went towards the temple. The light from the wayside lamps that lined the path commingled with the shadows. The sounds in the distance began to separate and become clear. The hawkers and shopkeepers by the road displayed many kinds of basins, pots, toys, chains and necklaces, flowers, mats and other things. Young girls stood in front of shops selling rouge and colour paste, their eyes shining with longing. The sellers called out to buyers, telling them about their wares. We passed them and reached the temple.

It was a small shrine with a centre stone. We went towards it and offered our salutations. One of the evening-lamp lighters at the shrine had kindled the sacred flame and was now singing songs to rouse the gods. The thammadi picked up one by one the pots filled with toddy and poured them on the centre stone. The liquid hit the stone, bubbled and ran down to the ground. The watching worshippers let out loud aarpu sounds and ululated.

Some of the uzhavar took us to the dining hall. Azhakan came, too. Cooked food that was ready to serve filled large basins, bowls and pots. The steam that rose from them brought alive appetizing scents – which wafted in the air. The children's nostrils widened. Their mouths were probably watering. Paraththa, the pleasure women who wore gold bangles and rings that gleamed on their fingers and fragrant night blooms in their hair, lingered around in small groups, laughing and joking with each other. Their nubile bodies that bore ripening breasts swayed seductively; so did the stolen glances of some young men which fell on them. The men loitered around them. There were so many kinds of people there – chaliyar, thunnalkkaar, kannaanmaar. There were also rich traders – the kadal vanikar and the koola vanikar. So many different sounds and laughter!

We were their guests. They led us to our seats. They served the children ghee rice and mutton. Pots of toddy were placed before the adults.

'We have fish curry and narumpizhi made from rice. Please eat to your heart's content!'

The heady aroma that rose up when the brew was poured from the pot into the cup left me elated.

'How do you make this?' I asked Azhakan, when my cup emptied in a second.

'I'll tell you,' he grinned. 'But it should stay a secret!'

'It can be made in many ways. This is how we do it: soak the rice, press it into balls, and dry it well in a large open-mouthed basin. Then add fragrant leaves of many kinds to it for one day and night. Then add the thaathirippoo, the flower that glows like fire, and also jaggery. You must stir the mixture well with your hands twice every day as you add the ingredients. Then pour the mixture into mud pots with narrow mouths, tie the mouths well with cloth and leave it for a long time. Finally, you have to pass it through a sieve of palm fibre made from strands cooked in boiling water.'

I noted down his instructions in my mind. Someday I have to try making this.

Once the spicy fish arrived, I must have emptied many more cups. For some reason, tears pricked at my eyelids. Mayilan and Chanthan, and the pain of our aimless wandering, must have swelled within me and flowed out through my eyes.

I wiped my eyes and reached out for another cup.

Azhakan stopped me gently. Enough, he said.

But I had another cup along with the dinner of mutton and rice. The heaviness of heart had subsided somewhat. But I was not drunk. Our women came over for their dinner. The uzhavar had kept munneer ready to offer – a mixture of palm juice, tender coconut water and sugarcane juice. They too finished dinner and stepped out. The munneer's gentle intoxication made some of them break into song. Their friends laughed and reminded them – that it was very late! We joined the uzhavar in the festivities again.

The merry sounds and happy sights drew us close. Some of our men too were eyeing the paraththa wenches. Young uzhavar men were still after them, I could see. I was surprised that their women were with them, but they still pursued the pleasure women openly!

The uzhavar cleared the space that had been readied for the dancing and music. We lowered our bundles. The humming and tapping sounds of our instruments as we prepared them attracted more people, who came over and stood around. The enthusiasm was infectious – our muzhavus and paras caught it quickly. We began by playing a maruthappann on our lutes. Ulakan picked up the karadika. When the slow opening beats began to give way to faster ones, the koothar's feet gained pace. The drumming grew into a great rolling surge. Chithira and Cheera began to sing. Perumpaanan played the periyaazh; we accompanied him with our lutes. The uzhavar cheered loudly – the meal of sumptuous narumpizhi and the clear, strong brew seemed to have raised their spirits.

The opening dance, the varikkoothu, was followed by the kuravakkoothu. Mukkannan danced the pandaarakkoothu, and Velan the thudikkoothu.

Chanthan was unmatched in his performance of both the pandaarakkoothu and the thudikkoothu. I remembered how those who saw him dance would remark that the very gods were dancing in him! Each of us felt his absence but did not show it. Some of the koothar dressed up as women and danced the pediyaadal; it made the spectators smile.

The eyes of our muzhavu drums remained open till dawn. The dancing and singing stretched on till daybreak. In the end, when the music of the lutes and the drums and the pipes began to climb towards a crescendo, Cheera began to whirl in frenzy, like a possessed one. It alarmed me. Her hair fell loose and flew about; sweat streamed down her forehead; her clothes were falling off. She did not wipe the sweat or retrieve her garment. The jasmine in her hair and the beads from her choker necklace were scattering all around. Her eyes were a coral red; they glinted in the light of the burning torch. Was this Cheera? Or the dead little girl who slept on her pyre with eyes open?

She looked inexhaustible. Indeed, it was as though her garments would turn into wings and she would fly away! My heart beat hard. When the music and the drumming reached their crescendo, she collapsed all of a sudden. Ulakan and I rushed to her. Nellakkili was screaming. We lifted her up. One of the uzhavar brought tender coconut water; we sprinkled some of it on her face and wetted her tongue with it. By the time she opened her eyes, the koothaattam was over. The paanar had played the puraneerma on their lutes, awakening the new day with praiseful prayer.

Seven

When we returned to the houses where we had spent the previous night, the eyes of the children there did not mirror suspicion any more. Instead, they were lit with awe and approval. They were still too shy to come near, but they really wanted to, one could see. I called out to them, smiling and clapping. For the little ones who overcame their shyness and ambled over, I made little flutes, making holes in pieces of bamboo. That attracted more of them.

Long reeds grew in the gardens of their houses, on which hung the vayala creepers with their green fruit. Tiny, reddish vayala saplings sprouted from under them. These were planted there by the householders to brew sweet liquor from their fruit. I cut some reeds that were not too tall, bored holes in them, and gave them to the children.

Azhakan and some other uzhavar came to us. Azhakan ran up to me and hugged me warmly. Last night's music and dance had fired them up. When I told them that we had to leave soon, he asked, why not stay on for a couple of days? Our Perumpaanan says, for love and respect to last, never tarry for long in places where you've danced and sung. I lovingly turned down their suggestion; they did not insist further.

I tried to get everyone together. Go after lunch then, the uzhavar said. Lunch was delicious steamed rice dumplings. The weariness from staying up all night was real, but when that potent brew from the night's feast was offered, I did not think twice about taking it. However, after three or four cupfuls, I stopped, remembering that too much of the brew would make walking during the day harder. I got up and began hurrying up the others.

'Where's Cheera? She wasn't here for lunch either?' asked Nellakkili, coming up to me. Fire leapt inside me. I jumped up, called out aloud for her, and ran outside. I had become aware of how her ways were changing. So my anxiety redoubled. We searched in the gardens and thickets nearby; she was nowhere to be found. The others too went in search of her in different directions. I went towards a thick clump of reeds where some children said they had seen her. It was hard to make my way through it as the creepers that grew wild on the reeds blocked me from entering. I did not think it likely that she would have taken this path, but I wanted to make sure that she hadn't. I called her name out aloud over and over, there was no response. Finally, struggling hard, I got through the dense clump and reached a pond. There she lay, eyes shut, on its lush green edge, one leg slipping into the water. I ran up to her and shook her hard, hauled her onto my lap and held her close. She opened her eyes.

'What happened, my daughter?' I cried. 'What happened to you?'

I concealed my shaken inner state. It could be known only by my quivering voice. I kissed her on the forehead.

She pointed towards the pond. I could see nothing there except the white lilies that bloomed amidst the tangles of vines and mulli plants.

'What is it there?'

'The crabs.'

'Did they pinch you?'

I peered at the water, alarmed.

The pond teemed with crabs. I checked her feet and legs. There were no pinch marks.

'I was watching the crabs. They were nipping off the new shoots of the vines. You can't tire watching them gather tiny grains of paddy from the fields and lug them to the cool mud-holes! It is a little scary, but you can't take your eyes off it!'

The words tumbled out of her mouth as though she had forgotten the world itself.

I too saw the speckled crabs on the muddy edge of the old pond overgrown with mulli plants and covered with their tangled roots. They were nipping at the water lilies.

'What happened to you then, my child? Tell me.'

'That I can't remember,' she said.

Pausing a moment, she continued: 'I'd stretched my hand out to pick some water lilies – the pond's so filled with them! Then I saw the crabs raise their pincers towards the lily stalks to pluck them. They have protruding eyes, like neem fruit, you know? Did you see this? The pictures they draw in the mud? So many things that I'd never seen before appeared and vanished in them! They came to life, they had bodies, I swear! These picture-things flitted about busily on the tangled vines and water-lily leaves. They made me feel quite dizzy! I can't remember anything after that.'

Aandavare, what was happening to this child!

My eyes filled with tears. I helped her stand up and then mounted her on my hip. Parting the clump of reeds, we moved ahead carefully. Monkeys pranced on the creepers, and it almost looked like they might bump against Cheera as they swung close. I covered her with the cloth around my waist and held her firmly. When we got out of the reeds and reached the courtyard of a house, the women came running towards us. The older children set off quickly in different directions to let the other search parties know.

I rested for a bit while Cheera was being fed by her mother. As usual, Nellakkili did not reveal her agony. But the searing pain she felt within was hurting me too.

When it seemed that Cheera had recovered for the most part, we hurried to resume our journey. Our

Perumpaanan bowed to the uzhavar respectfully. Mallika sang the maruthappann one more time. Her notes soared towards the sky, seeking the god Vendan's blessings. The uzhavar women had dressed well to bid us farewell. Their braided hair was adorned with garlands of jasmine. Some of them still held in their hands the reed containers filled with black kohl. They embraced our women warmly. Their kohl-rimmed eyes turned a sad, pale yellow; they must miss us so! The warmth that had sprung up between us over a single night left me a little astonished. They gave us a large packet of rice and meat to eat on the way. One of the uzhavar handed a rather big purse of coins to Perumpaanan.

'More than we agreed,' he said.

Perumpaanan bowed his head again in gratitude. They pointed to us the road to Parambumala. We promised Azhakan and the others that we would come again. I looked around for Cheera. She was standing by herself, oblivious of the world, in rapt attention at the sight of four gauzy-winged dragonflies. As we walked, she holding on to my finger, they darted around her.

The uzhavar were back at work in their fields by then. They were now manuring the fields cleared of weeds with kanchi flowers. Some of them hurried to trap the vaala fish that thrived in the water-filled fields. Their eyes reached us through the hazy blue

73

of the flowers that grew on the ridges of the field. All of them stood up and waved to us smilingly. We bowed to them and moved on. Then some uzhavar offered us bundles of string beans. Though it was not easy to add more to what we were already carrying, we did not refuse the gift. We bowed to them once again and continued on our path, crossing the fields and going beyond.

Now the path began to get crowded. Bullock carts passed us by. The bells on the necks of the animals rang. Because the path was even, the merchants who rode in them could doze a bit. The bullocks too were free of the fear of the whip and ran steadily. The crossroads bustled with people, and so it was easy to ask for the way. Now that we too had some coin, we felt somewhat proud. We felt that the shops beside the pillars near the shade trees by the road were also meant for us. If we needed something, we could buy it – that very feeling was exciting! We passed by fields and ponds – the homes of uzhavar in between; blacksmiths' forges; the workshops of bronze workers, the kannaanmaar; the silk weavers, the chaliyars, at their looms in front of their houses; the kuyiluvar, making drums and lutes.

'Take a look,' one of them called out to us. He had been checking the sounds of a para, and saw us by chance. 'No harm in looking!'

'We are in a hurry now, we will come over on our way back,' we shouted back – we wanted to avoid delay.

We had to reach Parambumala before nightfall. Everyone was making an effort, even the children, to walk fast, ignoring the fatigue from staying up all night. I felt a rush of love towards them all.

Parambumala, which had shone in the distance like a green gemstone, was near now. The flat paths of the plains had ended. The clear skies made the climb easy, but the children were beginning to tire. The flaming golden venga trees and the fragrant akil trees thrived on either side of the path uphill; they announced themselves to be a forest, but there was something bright and cheery about the place. Streams that seemed to yearn to be reborn as rivers . . . fields of millet . . . sights that added to that pleasant air. The distant hum of the wind in the bamboo clumps drifted into our ears. The peacocks which crouched behind the trees, the black monkeys that swung on the branches, the flocks of deer dancing in the meadows – all of them made us feel much less afraid of the wild.

The hills rolled ahead of us. The valley was covered with nochi flowers. The churappunna trees grew thickly together. From up there we could see the winding paths which we had climbed up. There were habitations in between, and so we met people on the road. We chatted with them and found out that they too were going to Parambumala. Some of these travellers were merchants going there to sell their goods. Others were like us, seeking Paari's generosity.

Paari is like the rain that falls alike on hill and stream, one of them praised him. We too felt that our desires may come true.

By the wayside were large, leafy, shady jack trees. Not just the children, but we adults were also hungry! We lowered our things in the shade of the trees and ate the meal of rice and meat that the uzhavar women had packed for us. Then some of us climbed the jack trees to pluck some ripe fruit; after we had our fill of the sweet, juicy flesh of the jackfruit, many felt that they could not walk a step further! We rested for a little while, when, all of a sudden, we heard a humming sound from a distance somewhere. It was coming towards us. Must be the rain, we thought. Sitting for long would only make us sluggish. So we got up and hurried on our way again.

It was not rain. When the noise grew near we realized that it was the hoof-beat of horses. It was a troop of soldiers. Seeing the wayfarers freeze with fear in their eyes, we knew that something was amiss.

'Looks like they are readying for battle,' someone said aloud.

'This is common here. The Vel Paari does not bow even to the Great Three. And who is not seduced by the boundless wealth of these lands?' another added.

'No one can defeat Paari in battle. The Great Three will have to retreat.'

Who knows what will happen! We began our climb again. The long walk had drained everyone, but no one begged to rest. It was the knowledge that we had to keep moving, even if we stumbled and stopped, that kept even the children going. Soon, we spotted the signs of a town on the hilltop. Little houses surrounded by thorn fences appeared on the wayside. Young girls were sweeping up the leaves of the eacha trees in front of their homes. They were scolding little children who were blowing at the tufts of cotton that had escaped their pods and now floated in the air. We had learned from our fellow travellers that bamboo, which needs neither plough nor hoe, was plentiful here, and so life was easier. Bamboo seed, jackfruit, yam and honey were abundant, and so the people lived without a care. Cows lay in cowsheds near the houses, chewing their cud placidly.

When we reached the town, the rising urge to reach our destination quickened our steps and narrowed our focus. We had to find out where Kapilar lived. We needed his kindness to learn more about Vel Paari. Someone on the road told us where his house was. It was near the king's palace, he said. We passed the busy sellers' street and that of the vellaalar to reach the grand houses where members of the king's retinue lived.

The sight of Vel Paari's grand palace made us feel bright and carefree. The eyes of our children, who had never seen anything like it, opened wide; they gazed in wonder. A large number of guards were stationed around the palace. Some of us retreated seeing them. They had probably noticed that we were just paanar and koothar and treated us like a common sight. But their sharp eyes fell on every other person there. Though a bit hesitant at first, I approached a guard and asked him where Kapilar's house was. He pointed to another imposing mansion, which was an exact copy of the second storey of the king's palace.

It was our insatiable eagerness that made us go in search of the poet up to the veranda of his house; he was not to be seen there. We waited for someone to turn up. The front yard was neatly kept. But we did not need help to recognize the person who appeared there a little later. There are some who need no introduction at all. Though not dressed splendidly, the wide forehead and the large eyes that gazed at all the world with a sense of wonder revealed who he was: the great poet. He gave us a quick glance, as though he knew why we were there. But not bothering to ask us anything, throwing us a hint of a smile, he hurried into the house.

Eight

We were left standing in front of that great house. Strips of palm leaf boiled in water were left to dry out on the front yard in the gentle sun. The breeze had blown them around. They were probably meant for the poet's pen. We looked at them; they seemed to make fun of us.

It was twilight. We had nowhere to go. When the poet came out to light the lamp, we were still standing outside his doorstep.

'Where do you come from? I can see that you are paanar and koothar. Do meet Vel Paari and tell him of your needs. He will surely help. I am a bit preoccupied.'

The voice sounded harsh, and so we hesitated to reply.

'You are right, master. We are indeed paanar and koothar. But we are not here to beg. We came here having heard of this place from Paranar, whom you know. It is he who told us to also meet you,' I said.

Kapilar was silent for a few moments.

'I am merciful to beggars too,' he then said. 'That is what I have learned from Paari . . . I was wrong to behave badly towards those who are masters of music and dance.'

Words that seemed to beg pardon. No, no need . . . our Perumpaanan joined his palms in salutation.

Kapilar continued: 'You are people who came here on Paranar's direction. Though not born of the same womb, he is dearer to me than a sibling. He was the first of my mentors. A master of song, compassionate and just.'

'Of that, we too have partaken much,' I said.

'All who are close to him will surely know,' he said. 'I remember the last time I saw him. At the mansion of

Vaiyavikko Perum Pekan. It is common for poets to follow generous chiefs.'

I sharpened my ears. It was of course important to learn of kings and chiefs who gave liberally to the needy for fame and honour.

'It was Pekan who raised Paranar to glory, ending his penury. Pekan's fame is such that he is known to have once given away his cloak to a peacock which seemed to be shivering from the cold! But this king left his queen Kannagi for another. That Pekan who showered mercy on everyone would not show it to his faithful wife greatly dismayed Paranar. He dared to say that Pekan was wrong. I echoed his words. Paranar will not flinch if the king does something wrong. He will speak up.'

He stopped, probably sensing that he could never talk enough of Paranar.

'Let it be! I will do whatever I can for you. You have had a long and tiring journey. Rest well today. You can be comfortable here. In Paari's land, singers and dancers will not starve. I am caught up in something unavoidable today. Let us meet tomorrow.'

The wick of the lamp grew darker the more it burned. Kapilar tapped it. He then summoned a helper.

'Penga, take care of these people. Make sure they have all they need.'

He saluted us again with folded hands and went inside.

'There is a large rest house that the king has built for travellers. You can stay there.'

We prepared to leave with Pengan, picking up the bundles that we had lowered earlier. Suddenly, I glimpsed someone come out of the house with quick steps. Something assailed me within, and for a few moments I stood there, struck dumb and unable to move even a finger. The figure vanished into the dim light of the street. I was still motionless.

'What happened?' Nellakkili hurried to my side.

'Nothing . . . Who was that who went out just now? Wasn't it our Mayilan?'

Nellakkili started.

'Mayilan? Really? It was so dark, I didn't notice him. How can he be here?'

'It has been years since we last saw him. Would you recognize him today at the very first glance? Maybe you are imagining it. Because you think of him all the time.'

Though she said this, I could see in her eyes a certain shine from years ago.

'Is it him?'

'Oh, gods! Let it be him!'

Our hearts beat together. Our inner worlds turned over restlessly as we walked with our people holding on to our things. I lost my sense of time and place. We reached the rest house and settled down again.

'Friend, who was the person who stepped out of the poet's house when we were getting ready to leave?' I asked Pengan.

'Many people come to see the poet. We don't get to know their names or where they are from. Today, too, there were many visitors.'

Then he seemed to delve into his memory.

'Wasn't it Chami who went out when we started from the house? Yes. Chami, it was. He comes often. He is close to the poet.'

I could not ask more. There were many other groups of paanar and koothar in the rest house, from many places. There was plenty of meat-rice, mutton and fresh toddy for everybody. We handed the caretakers the bundles of string beans. Everyone ate well. The children fell into an exhausted slumber. Though we had found a safe place to rest, I could not get sleep for a long time. Was it Mayilan that we saw? What news would Chanthan bring? This land was new to us, but something seemed to be crouching in the dark. I had nightmares even in that half-sleep – of termites that bore into living eyes that were wide open.

All of us woke up quite late. The trying walk after the long night of singing and dancing had indeed been very tiring. We felt no more the urgency to seek the generosity of the great. We bathed in a stream outside, returned refreshed for a meal of cooked millet and sour curry with curds, and stepped out.

Though we had slept well and had had a hearty meal, we were not sure whether to go to Kapilar's house or not. No one had come from there seeking us. The poet must be very busy. He would send for us later. So we did not go to him; instead, we took a walk around and went back to the rest house. My eyes searched for just one face, but we did not see it. I wanted to go to Kapilar's house once again to look for Chami, but I was not sure how the poet would react, so I held myself back. We continued to stay in the rest house and walk around in the town from time to time.

Two days passed thus. Though we had found a place to stay, the worry about how we were to carry on in the days ahead began to consume us again. We were at the rest house with nothing to do, when Pengan came over.

'The poet asks you to come and meet him.'

Our hearts brightened. We got ready quickly and followed him. Kapilar was seated in front of his house. Seeing us, he smiled.

'Come, come,' he welcomed us. 'I was very busy these past two days. I could not even see you. How is the food there? Have you been able to rest?'

My eyes searched for Chami. Was he here?

Before we could reply, Kapilar said, 'You must see Vel Paari tomorrow. I have arranged for everything with the palace guards. You must be ready with songs that celebrate him.'

Our Perumpaanan cleared his throat to say something. Then he decided against it.

'Master, we know nothing about Vel Paari. Paranar said you would tell us . . .' I said.

Kapilar burst out laughing.

'The thing is to rid ourselves of want . . . it does not matter of whom one sings praises, or how, isn't it? Yes, it is true. For those who seek a livelihood through their singing, this is about making a living. Indeed, you need to think of how you can make a living out of song and dance.'

The poet paused a moment and continued.

'Vel Paari is very powerful. There was a time when the Mighty Three would break into a cold sweat at just the mention of his name. He has a great army of spear-wielders and elephants, and he does not flinch from face-to-face combat. He controlled three hundred villages once. Those, he donated to paanar and the indigent who sought refuge in him. Now all he has is this hill and the town on the hilltop. If anyone begs him for it, he might give it away too! You have seen how the land is, how the people are. For songsters these details will be more than enough.'

Even when he said this, I detected a faint quiver in the poet's tone.

'But Paari's strength is also his weakness. God relents, irrespective of your offering – it could be just an erikku flower or a leaf of the koovalam tree. The gods do not discriminate between flowers that can be and can't be worn. This Vel is the same.'

Paari, Paari, Paari! The poets sing
Eloquent lines of fulsome praise
And from it the very earth they gain!
But it is not only Paari who nurtures the world
It is nourished also by the rain!

The poet hummed a song he had written about Paari for us. When we were about to leave, he told us: 'I will send Pengan to you tomorrow. Go with him and meet the Vel. And . . . wait . . .' He went inside and brought some palm-leaf pages, handing them to us. Perumpaanan looked at me, and I took them, stretching my hands out respectfully. I tucked them away safely in the small packet I held.

On the way back to the rest house, I went over every single word that the poet had uttered. There were thorns strewn among them; they disturbed me. I tried to hum some lines. But the swirling currents in my restless heart were dripping into my lines and tunes; I gave up and went along with the others.

My mind did not clear up even after we reached the rest house. Perumpaanan was also humming some lines. He seemed unperturbed. His tranquil, mellow bearing always fascinated me. I opened the palm-leaf pages that the poet had given us and began

85

to read. It was his kurinjhi song. Parambumala with its trees, birds and flowers and its people rose up before my eyes.

In one of the songs, the names of many flowers were threaded in, like a long chain. I read it out to Cheera: kaanthal, aambal, anicham, kuvala, kurinjhi, vedchi, kalli, kooviram, vaaka, kutacham, eruva, cheruvila, karuvilam, payini . . . she counted ninety-nine names. I could see the whole of a gentle summer wake up in her. It brightened my mind. When I lay down to sleep at night, I too had threaded together a few lines.

We woke up early the next morning. Perumpaanan and Chithira were already rehearsing some songs. Everyone joined to rehearse each song. The koothar were practising movements and poses and steps. When Pengan came, we were working at remembering each song correctly. We had sung and danced only for the people; never had we performed for a ruler. The fear that we might be ruined if this went wrong – it dogged me.

We reached Paari's abode. Pengan walked ahead of us. The pillars of that spacious palace were of solid granite. The upper storey was resplendent with many kinds of decorations. In the sprawling audience hall inside, under curtains of blue silk, sat Paari on the royal couch, verily like the God of the Sky. We needed no one to tell us who he was. When we bowed low to him, he stood up and raised his hand.

'You are here on Kapilar's word! What more do we need to be convinced that you possess great talent?'

That made our hearts pound hard.

'Please forgive us if what we say is improper . . . we have never performed before the mighty . . . We are here only because of the mercy shown to us by the great poet Kapilar. Please pardon us if we make a mistake . . .'

Paari smiled and raised his hand, as if ordering us to begin.

We spread out with our lutes and drums. Kapilar was not there, nor was Chami. I handed Perumpaanan the lute of twenty-one strings and prepared my own. We began with invocations to the divine – the orottuvaarum and the eerottuvaarum. Then Perumpaanan, Chithira and I sang a song of praise, extolling the Vel.

Hail, Paari, who, with the curve of his bow
Presses down now this proud land's brow!
Land, which relents to wetness alone,
Wetness that wells from within its own.
Land, which till now succumbed to none,
This land, it now submits to the One!
Hail Paari! Hail, hail!

The song was over, but we did not feel brave enough to look up at Paari. The koothar were preparing to perform the akakkoothu. The elleri, aakuli and thatta drums, and the kuzhal pipes, were ready. The koothar danced the kocham and the meikkoothu. It seemed to me that everything was being done exactly as it should be. After the perfectly executed akakkoothu, the king ordered us to dance some pieces from the purakkoothu. Make sure that the beats and poses of the akakkoothu and the purakkoothu don't get mixed up, the koothar whispered to each other. The virali women danced the kuravakkoothu. It was followed by the varikkoothu; the whole performance became lively.

With the music gaining in tempo, the onlookers began to join in. The koothar murmured among themselves that these newcomers were going to ruin the steps and the rhythm, but we did not stop them. When the dance went completely out of step, I began to wonder – what has this become, a chaotic veriyaattam? Perumpaanan and I exchanged glances and silently agreed to end the performance. When we wrapped up the performance with salutations to the ruler and to the gods, Vel Paari looked very pleased. He got up.

My eyes and heart both felt full and cooled. When a dance is over, it should leave behind a desire for more in the audience!

'You clearly know music and dance in and out,' said Paari. 'I do not know what will be a sufficient reward! Tell me without hesitation, what is it that you want?'

Perumpaanan bowed low in deep gratitude. He had barely cleared his throat to speak when a voice sounded behind him: 'Give us this realm! We want this land!'

Perumpaanan and I staggered in shock. Everyone who heard it reeled with surprise. That voice belonged to someone who had joined the dance towards the end. Vel Paari looked completely stunned. Before we could stop them, some people who were standing beside us moved up.

'Be kind enough to bestow the realm that you rule upon us.'

The guards and the soldiers rushed ahead to block their way. But Paari stopped his guards.

'I have never hesitated to give away whatever I have to others. But this is deceit. Who are you? Tell me the truth!'

We realized that we too had been betrayed, like Paari. But we could not utter a word.

'You are known to shower wealth on completely unknown people, then why do you need to know?'

One of those who threw the challenge stepped forward a little.

'I will grant anything to those who can sing and dance; I will hold up the indigent and the poor. But I will not suffer traitors!'

His eyes, which had been moist with mercy before, now blazed with anger.

'We are taking over this realm! The palace is surrounded. If you value your life, surrender!'

Paari drew his sword and faced his opponents. He took a couple of steps – but the brave Vel was cut down from behind and fell. It was by his own – I saw no more. The hall now rang with ugly screams and snarls. There was no way to make out friend or foe. I called out to my people and rushed out. Our women ran after us, screaming. Some tried to stop us; others tried to let us pass. When I got out of the palace, I saw that my body was bathed in blood. I could not run any more; I collapsed.

Many people jumped over my body and dashed away. One of them turned back to look at me. Was it Chami? No, Mayilan! No matter how many years pass, I can recognize my son.

My people were now around me. Cheera and Chithira and Nellakkili were sobbing and crying out. I pointed to Mayilan, but before they could look, he had disappeared in the melee.

'Nellakkili,' I said, 'that is our Mayilan!'

Then a white shroud covered my eyes. Except for the screams that rang all around me, I remember nothing after that.

II
Chithira

One

'Ah! Kolumba! My right wing is broken!'

Our Perumpaanan wailed, but Achan did not respond. Ulakan and the others managed to carry him back to the rest house. He kept asking for Mayilan. Perumpaanan had tried to bandage the wound on his chest with his waist cloth not long after Achan fell, but the blood kept seeping out. The wound was deep.

The rest house was empty when we got back there. Perumpaanan went out with Ulakan and brought back some medicinal roots and leaves. They were crushed, mixed with fat from goat's milk and white mustard, and applied to the wound. Erava and neem leaves were collected and placed on the veranda. I was told to build a fire a little distance away to burn akil leaves for their fumes.

Amma kept swabbing Achan's wound. While I made the fire, Perumpaanan played the kaanchippann on Mallika. I could not stop my tears when I heard Achan's Mallika sing, pleading for his life. We did not make sense of all that Perumpaanan told us to do; we just followed his directions. Cheera was in a world of her own. Though silent, the upheaval and murmurs and emptiness in her mind did flash on her face now and then. Her inner world, however, was inscrutable.

Those who were staying in the rest house had left by then. They had carried away most of the things there. We did not have anything left to eat even. Most of us were scared to step out. Because we were used to hunger, we stayed in for a couple of days. Maybe we forgot to eat – so numb we were with the shock of what had happened. Later, some among us began to creep out, mostly at night. We went to the hill slopes and returned with yams and jackfruit.

There was no way to go to the town during the day; nor could we trust anyone. It was possible that the people too distrusted us. The soldiers chased us away whenever they saw us. Some of us who went out there were attacked by a mob. They called us traitors. We tried to run and hide, but it was useless. They beat us up; some fell on the ground under the blows. Others beseeched the attackers with folded hands, crying out tearfully that we were innocent. They stopped only when some of their own dissuaded them – we were by then cowering at their feet, wailing and weeping, telling them again and again of our blamelessness. There is a song which speaks of the paanar cutting off the strings of their lutes as they mourned the death of Evvy, the chieftain of a land named Mizhalakkuttam. But at Paari's death, not just the lute but its player himself was cut down – one of us, a living man, stabbed in the breast. We were not traitors. We would not suffer that slur.

The women should not go out, our men said. We had heard that the traitorous soldiers had barged into the inner courtyards of Paari's abode and had dragged out his consorts by their hair, robbing them of their jewels and tearing their garments. The tears of the women of a fallen land add to the punch of victory, it seems! There was talk that the millet fields had been set on fire, goats and cattle seized, and people butchered.

Even the memory of what had happened right in front of our eyes made us quiver in fright. Just the mention of song and dance made us break into tears. We longed for the old days when we were all together despite the neediness and distress! No, we shouldn't have set out at all. To be trapped in a foreign land with no friends! Achan was wounded in body and heart; will he return to us? No – I would feel sometimes. And then I hated the hardness of heart which told me that.

Kapilar was drowning in grief at Paari's death, we heard. The poor man! Paari had two daughters, they said. Now they were orphans. The talk was that Paari's murder by treachery was planned by the Mighty Three, together. No one offered the girls refuge because they feared the great powers. Kapilar now looked after the girls. These were the bits of news our men brought back when they returned; really, we knew nothing much of what was happening outside. I didn't want to learn more either. Our presence must have been upsetting to the lives of the people here, like discordant notes that hurt a melody. We must have been beyond their understanding … like pages full of strange words.

Ulakan kept saying that we should go to Kapilar. One evening, after it was dark, he tried to go there, but the house was surrounded by soldiers. He came back at once. He meant to find some information about Chami, besides seeing the poet. Was that Annan? I had only a vague memory of him; I was very young when he left. And Amma did not see him at the gate of Kapilar's house. But Achan kept moaning, calling out for him; each time she heard him, Amma's eyes welled up. It tore at me from within; I wept away from her sight.

Achan must have seen someone else. If it really was Annan, why did he stay away? Why would he run away so coolly, like a stranger, barely looking at the man who had given him life, lying on the ground wounded? I felt no urge to seek out Chami. Chanthan would find out about Annan from Ezhimala or elsewhere. They would come back together. Our people knew this, but were still anxious to know more about Chami. My anxiety was all about Achan. Or maybe that sorrow just drowned out everything, brimming over all else.

Our wait was in vain; Perumpaanan's medicinal balm was powerless to hold back Achan's spirit. It flew away on the fifth day after he was wounded. Music and dance must have already relinquished his body by then. Amma's boundless sorrow, pressed down within her for too long, now gushed into the open in a flood of wails and tears. Ulakan and Cheera, who had never seen her lament, hugged her close. I was numb. Everything seemed to be unfolding at a distance. When you are in a place where you have no one, living and dying feel like the same.

We made for him the last bed of palm grass. We sang to the gods, begging them to show him the way from the earthly realm to the realm of the sky. Perumpaanan, who stood nearest to his pyre, in front of everyone else, whispered, as though to himself, that the spirit that had left the body and mounted the flames had now become a being of the sky. Even then he must have felt the void left by a severed right wing. All sorts of voids swirled around me. Achan was a man in whom kindness and knowledge had come together; the very core of music had been revealed to him. But what did he achieve in this world? It takes death to lay bare the fact that each of us who seem to be bound together are in truth alone.

Seeing Amma with her tresses cut and bangles cast off, I could not help thinking – maybe she would have been better off ascending the pyre with Achan.

What to do now? Staying here was impossible. We should return to our native land. Yes, there would be need and privation, but we would not wander aimlessly! The possibility that floating adrift like this could pull us deeper into the vortex of pain made me feel very afraid.

I minced no words when I told Perumpaanan what I thought. He did not respond. But after a long pause, he whispered – we should meet Kapilar one more time. He seemed to be telling that to himself but it was meant for me too. Ulakan too felt that we needed the poet's help if we were to leave this land unscathed; I agreed with him. But they could not meet Kapilar.

Two more days passed thus; then, quite unexpectedly, one of the poet's helpers came over to the rest house. Perumpaanan invited him to come in, but he preferred to stand outside. The ruin of the land showed in his wilted and sad mien. The vigour and happiness in his words had dried up.

The great poet Kapilar had left Parambumala. He had taken the two daughters of Paari with him as there was no one who would protect them in this land. Before he left, he had told his helpers that his aim was to find good matches among the princes of the lands for the young princesses so that they would be safe.

Perumpaanan could only listen to him without a word. The ground beneath our feet was crumbling, stone by stone. We faltered in every step as we walked.

98

'I came to tell you something else,' the man said. 'This place is not safe for you any more. You must start immediately. It is going to be difficult for you to get out of Parambumala. So a group of guards will come with you till you get past this land. The master had arranged for this before he left.'

So the great poet had remembered us before he left . . . I felt tears prick at my eyelids. May life be good to the girls he protects, I prayed.

'Then we will start immediately!'

We hurried to pack our things. This land, famed for bestowing riches on even beggars, had given us nothing but never-ending agony. We struggled to lighten the load of pain that kept swelling within us.

Kapilar's helper had left. The guards were waiting for us when we came out of the rest house. Flanked by them, we began to descend the hill. The houses on either side of the path looked still and deserted. Their front yards were overgrown with weeds and smothered by fallen eacha leaves. Cotton pods seemed to have burst everywhere, and tufts of cotton floated sadly in the air. The girls who live there must be now cowering in fear and sadness inside their houses, watching us leave.

I kept turning my head back, searching for something. We had joined a beloved one to the earth here, and were now leaving callously. Though we walked away from the hill, it still appeared close.

'Achan is coming with us!'

Amma did not have the strength to turn back and look when Cheera said that. The faint breeze tried to lift up the garment's edge with which she had covered her shaved head. When it shifted to reveal her scalp with clumps of hair still sticking out here and there on it, she fought off the breeze. I shuddered as I remembered her tresses.

'Why chop off a woman's femininity when her man passes?'

Cheera seemed to read my mind. Or maybe we just thought that at the same time. She had got past childhood quickly. Now she trod on paths that grown people feared to enter.

'Who made all these customs? If you listen to the older folk, you might think that they just bloomed on their own, like flowers on trees!'

'Chechi, do you know the song of the woman who got ready to climb on her husband's pyre?'

No, I shook my head.

Oh wise ones, oh wise ones!
You will not let me leave,
You will not let me die!
Oh wise ones so full of wile . . .

Cheera sang softly. The wise poets declared that a widow did not have to end her life, entering her husband's funeral pyre. But she knew that this was not kindness; it was cruelty. A woman who loses her man should either follow him without delay or blister and burn every moment, die inch by inch.

'Sing all of it,' I told her.

Cheera pretended that she was recalling the lines and softly sang the rest of her song.

> *See, I am not the girl*
> *Who yearns for the oblong cucumbers*
> *with curved lines running on them like squirrels' backs,*
> *I am not the girl who longs for*
> *chopped bland cucumbers . . .*

Whoever wrote that song is firm of word, I thought, approvingly. She is making fun of the pitiless poets; she is taking revenge on them through her own death.

> *I am not the girl who'll*
> *Stay a lifetime on the hard and naked floor.*
> *I am not the girl who'll*
> *Quietly eat the leftover rice*
> *Dry without a drop of ghee*
> *Served with a meagre*
> *Vela leaf curry, sour with tamarind*
> *And the paltry sesame chutney . . .*

Cheera groped for the rest of the lines inside her head – then we heard someone sing in a low voice behind us and stopped. '*With black pieces of firewood . . .*' the song which Cheera began was threaded further. It was Amma. We had forgotten that she was very near. The song continued, as though it would not end, though Cheera had stopped singing.

> *At the sight of this pyre of black wood*
> *Lit in the wild of this crematory*
> *You must flinch within,*
> *But I am the woman of my man,*
> *My broad-shouldered husband.*
> *I am not afraid!*
> *The pond filled with blooming lotuses,*
> *Brimming with cool water —*
> *And the burning flames are now, to me,*
> *The same.*

Amma's voice did not break even as she sang. Was she weeping? Those around us must also be searching for tears on her face. I knew well that she would never give in to those who were convinced that she was born to weep. I have been proud that I am as strong of heart as she is. But now when I looked at her, I doubted if my decision would have been the same as hers; it made me feel guilty. Descending the heights is always harder than ascending the slopes.

We neared the valley.

'You are out of danger now,' said one of the guards. 'We will take leave from you now.' Only then did it strike me that nothing untoward had happened.

Perumpaanan approached them reluctantly as they turned to leave.

'Please stop for a moment . . . we are not learned enough to make sense of what happened there . . . but we would like to know . . .'

The guards stopped. Perumpaanan continued, his voice trembling: 'Can you please tell us, who made pawns of us? Can we please know that at least before we leave?'

'All of us are mere pawns, Ayya! What do we know of the games played by kings? Even that which is clear to the eye is unclear to the mind!'

They could say no more. Perumpaanan saw that. He did not persist. We bowed to them and walked onwards, not knowing where to go.

Two

'Are we going back to our motherland?' Ulakan asked. 'Are we returning to the place that gave us life?'

All we knew was that we were descending from Parambumala; we had no idea where we were bound for. Most of us had assumed that we were going back home. It was only now that someone actually put the thought into words.

'What else to do?' asked Perumpaanan wanly. 'Go to another king? Witness yet another turmoil and the trampling down of a place and its people? There is a saying that if the ones who never laugh actually laugh on a special day, that day will cease to be special! We are jinxed, we will be the ruin of the people there!'

We had never heard Perumpaanan utter such bitter, sad words. Seeing how heavy his heart was, we were silent for some time.

Then Ulakan turned to Perumpaanan, 'If we are going back home, how are we to live? Wasn't it you who told us that there is no greater misfortune than poverty?'

There was truth in Ulakan's words. He seemed to have matured in word and deed after Achan's passing. He now filled on his own a void so big that no one had thought it could ever be filled. But there is no such thing as a void, actually. All empty spaces are inevitably filled by something else sooner or later. That is the rule of life. It never fails.

'What am I to say, my child?' Perumpaanan replied. 'We are now less than what we were when we set out. Even our limbs seem to be falling off . . .'

'I have heard that poverty and riches turn like the surfaces of a wheel, that they follow one another, and that even great wealth is not exempt from this rule. If that is true, we will be blessed by good times someday, won't we?'

Ulakan's innocence brought the brightness back to Perumpaanan's face. But he did not speak; he just listened.

'We must raise ourselves up from hardship. Find out about Chami. Locate Annan. Wait for Chanthan who went looking for him. How can we return without finishing any of these?' Ulakan reminded us. 'It may be something that stretches back to an earlier birth – but we must still finish the task. Remember, when we set out we had vowed to return only after we tried our best.'

Most of us supported Ulakan. Perumpaanan seemed to have no objection, but his words were apathetic.

'Not easy to find another king to lean on. Let us go to some land where coin and wealth are plenty. Let us be satisfied with what we can earn from whatever work we can find.'

'All we know is to sing and dance. And now all we have are feet with no ankle bells and lutes with broken strings . . .'

My words made everyone feel despondent again. I should not have uttered them, I thought. And so I decided to say something else.

'In that case, where do we go? Why not go to the uzhavar's lands? They have money, don't they?'

'No, let us not go there. They are rich. We are poor. We may be able to earn our keep each day, but we will not be their equals in their eyes. We will forever be receiving their charity.'

People began to separate the chaff from the grain of whatever they had heard. In the end, Perumpaanan decided: 'Let us not retreat. We will go somewhere else and find a place where we can settle. The land which we reach will be our homeland.'

For those who have no destination, any path will do. They have no worries about getting lost! In every place we passed we looked for signs: Will it suit us? Will we thrive? We searched each other's faces and knew when it wasn't the right place. There were even and uneven roads. Steep climbs and descents. We lost all sense of time as we walked on. We ate the fruit of jack trees and mango trees growing on the wayside; drank our fill from the water fountains near the roads. We kept walking.

The day was almost over. No habitations were visible anywhere. The road that lay ahead was reddish, the colour of the chenkaanthal flower. The red of the road was flanked on both sides by the abundant green of wild bushes. People began to worry about the halt at night. It was impossible to walk, anyway. Our legs had grown heavy. When it felt that my body would defy me and act on its own, I sat down on the ground. Seeing me, the others – not just the children, but also the adults – began to sit down on the stones and in the shade of the thettaa trees.

Beyond the thickets we saw the rolling meadows, like a sea of green. The heads of mating couples of the small-horned erala deer and young chamari deer bobbed up and down in it. They pressed on each other's bodies, and their heads seemed to flow on the green waves in the sea of grass. We saw flocks of cattle returning at dusk; it certainly seemed that there was a settlement somewhere near.

'Let's walk a bit more when you are less tired,' Perumpaanan suggested, hiding his worry about finding a safe resting place for the night. There may indeed be such a place this night, it seemed. I got up and went along with the others. We followed the cattle, somehow managing to drag our tired legs along.

We were not wrong. Flocks of cattle from all over were returning to an open space where men had gathered. They were not in a hurry to separate their own animals, which stood crowding in a corner. There was a small platform raised under a konna tree and someone was sitting on it. The golden blooms of the konna had fallen all around him. The audience stood in rapt attention, listening to what he had to say. This was the village headman, and he was delivering a judgment on some dispute.

Perumpaanan suggested that we wait till this was over.

Only then did we notice a young woman standing in the middle of the crowd with swollen, reddened, sad eyes, which looked as though they had no more tears to shed. Her hair was in disarray; so also her attire, draped carelessly on her thin body. She seemed oblivious to all that was going on. An older woman stood next to her, complaining loudly. This was obviously her mother. She was pointing accusingly towards a young man who stood at a distance. He was pretending ignorance, feigning surprise.

We got to know what the matter was when we listened to her. This young man had been frequenting their home at night secretly, visiting her daughter. But for all these secret visits, he didn't seem to want a life with her. The mother did not know what had happened between the two. When the girl grew thinner and thinner, she thought that some evil spirit had possessed her; she even tried holding a veriyaattu to get rid of it. She vowed to do many kinds of worship if her daughter got better. In the end, when she learned that the girl was in love, she went and met the young man. Though she begged him to accept her daughter, he would not budge. She then implored him to spend a single night with her daughter with the knowledge of his loved ones; he refused even that. He was apparently getting ready to abandon her and leave the place in search of wealth. The mother, when she heard this, had rushed to the village headman with her grievance.

The village headman ordered the young man to take the girl's hand.

'You are young, my children,' he said. 'We cannot approve of the deceit that creeps in and out at night – we are for true and faithful love that shines in the open! Our sacred ariviyals say that those who build lives as householders are above the ascetics and the gods themselves! Those who imbibe in their hearts what is necessary to know, those who shun what they must shun, and do what they must do will never fail. My daughter, let me tell you something. Love is the very path of the spirit, of life. But even a loving man may at times be cruel. Forgive him, remember his love. If you cannot, then you must indeed leave him. May that not happen!'

Her situation disturbed me. A mismatched marriage can only be endless pain. One can have no faith in a skirt-chaser of a man. If he fancies another woman, he will leave his wife. And she will spend the rest of her life seething in pain. All this is common.

The village assembly had ended. Neither the young man's face nor the girl's face had brightened. It was apparent that discord and friction that would last a lifetime had already begun. Her life may now become a garment that unravelled bit by bit with each wash.

Perumpaanan approached the village headmen. Some of our senior men were with him. We needed the kindness of these people to stay the night. We waited without setting our bundles down.

Perumpaanan came over to us.

'They are kind folk. Mostly kovalar, cowherds who live day to day. And treat others just like their own blood. They say that we can join them.'

Good, even if it is just for a day, everyone agreed.

'Maybe we shouldn't stay for more than a day. We may be exploiting their goodness,' Ulakan reminded us.

The idayar were waiting for us; they led the way as we followed them. They chatted with us as though they had known us for long. We told them about all that had befallen us. We could see their easy friendliness turn into kindness and consideration.

These people were generous and warm. Maybe this was the refuge we had been seeking for so long!

We were led into a settlement with rows of little huts with thatched roofs. Konna trees grew near the huts, casting their shade on them. Vines of pichaka flowers grew in plenty in the small front yards of these homes. The idaya women hurried out of their homes and invited us in, greeting us with big smiles. Their huts were tiny, with barely enough space for their families – we noticed right then. These were people who would not complain about having very little; were we doubling their troubles?

We lingered outside, in the open space that connected all the little homes. When they urged us in again, we ventured in reluctantly. The floors and walls were plastered with cow dung. Leather hides and cowherds' sticks hung on the walls. Pot holders with bronze pots hung down from the roof. The rooms were small, but scrupulously clean. From the railings of the fence at the back of the houses, one could see the lengthy cowsheds. Behind them was a long row of kanchi trees.

I beckoned to the young girls in skirts with pretty markings of colour paste on their breasts, their long hair in braids. A little one ran to me eagerly with a toothy smile. Her teeth flashed a pearly white, like jasmine buds. I held her close. She was from next door; Taramma's daughter. The older women were busy cooking for us. We took in everything: the sound of the rice cooking in the pot bubbling up. The wonderful scent of rabbit meat and beef curries wafting in from nearby houses.

Seated in rows on the wide open space in front of the huts, we ate with relish a hearty meal of ghee rice, meat curry and curds. The food was served by broad-shouldered women. I noticed that none of the older men were present. When we women were sitting around and chatting after supper, I asked one of the idaya women why that was so.

'We idayar are not all alike,' she told me. 'Not in trades or wealth. We are the poor and so live in these small settlements. There are rich folk here, many of them. They have a lot of cattle – plenty of cows and goats and buffaloes! They keep pearls and gold coins in their mansions. Our men take turns to guard these houses. Those who leave for guard duty can return only after daybreak.'

I was amazed. What you see from afar may not be what you see from near. Many kinds of people! Their ways are so different. Kindness and cruelty are the two faces of the same heart, and they shade into each other. You may be seeking one, but it may be the other that you stumble on. One cannot trust everyone.

But I chided myself immediately for harbouring such a suspicion about these undoubtedly warm and giving folk. I tried to wipe it away from my mind. Some lively young girls ran up to me to ask if I'd like to dance the kuravakkoothu with them. I was very tired and so I refused lovingly. The women laid out a mat for me inside the house. Our men slept on the verandas.

People of many kinds. And lives, too . . . I must have thought of such things before I fell asleep.

Three

When we got ready to leave the next morning, the kovalar stopped us. That was probably because they knew that we had nowhere to go. We had told them of our predicament the night before. Not that we were keen to go. But it felt wrong to subsist forever on the generosity of others – we wanted to work and to earn our keep. We were not sure if there were people here who needed that which we could provide – dance and music.

It appeared that the kovalar had given more thought to these aspects than we had. A few things had already been discussed with the village headman. Perumpaanan went with the kovalar to see him. He returned soon with good news. Not only were we allowed to settle in this land, but the people here would help us get together all that we needed.

By evening that day, five huts with thatched roofs were erected a little distance away from the settlement which had first given us refuge. The money that we had earned from the uzhavar was spent on buying utensils for the kitchens and rice. We tried to pay the kovalar for the milk and curds they gave us, but they refused.

'The season of bullfights is going to start,' some of them let Perumpaanan know. 'You won't have to remain idle! Also, there are many wealthy folks around here. They'll have dance and music for the ceremonies at their houses and for the festivals that we hold in common.'

'Of course we know this is nothing . . . you have had to walk on burning coals! But still, please tell us what you need, anything! We can't gift you great wealth, but surely, we can make your lives free of care.'

Perumpaanan sighed. What words of gratitude could he possibly offer these people who were holding out the gift of life itself to us? Maybe the words did not form in his mind, so he just bowed low and folded his palms in deep respect. My eyes moistened. Yes, most of the people we had met till now were kind. But hardship had been our most abiding companion.

I would finish my chores at home during the day and go over to visit the kovalar's homes. The girls there became my friends. They too were very busy, but we got together whenever we could. All three of them – Pachakkili, Thaamara and Kiliyolam – were good singers. Kiliyolam would play the lute made from the stick-like fruit of the konna tree, and when she pressed her lips on it, it looked as though she was rising up into the sky. In the few days that I had spent with them, they too must have heard me sing some songs! On the nights when the men went off to serve as guards, the older women would join us to sing kuravakkoothu songs. Cheera would come with me to visit our friends sometimes. Mostly she stayed at home and kept Amma company.

The older idayar men would go off to graze their cattle in far-off meadows. The older children would go around the houses of other people and the marketplaces selling milk, curd, butter and buttermilk. I was closest to Kiliyolam; one day I went along with her to sell curd. The idayar houses were not alike. Some had large herds of goats. In others, the cowsheds were so long and big that you couldn't make out where the cowshed ended and the house began. In the smaller houses, they'd have just two or three cows, but the houses of the wealthy with large cowsheds had many animals. Many hands were hired to care for them. Inside the bull pens were huge, angry bulls which looked as though they were itching for a fight, kicking the ground impatiently and making deep hoof marks in the wet mud. They challenged each other constantly and even wounded each other.

'It is not easy to take care of these beasts. The ordinary workers won't do. You need young fellows, and they have to be skilled bullfighters,' said Kiliyolam. The sight of these huge creatures with massive tangled tufts falling on their faces left me dumbstruck. Their enormous bodies were streaked with blood. Some young kovalar men were trying to separate the ones which had locked horns. The bull-keepers who tried to move the brutes out of the pens so that they could be tied up somewhere else were not spared either – they too were bruised badly and blood seeped from their wounds. Others were trying to calm down seemingly untameable bulls by tethering cows near them.

'This work . . . you could lose your life any time doing it, right?' I felt sorry for those young men.

'Sometimes the bulls gore them with their horns, their very entrails get pulled out . . .' Kiliyolam lowered her voice: 'This happened some time back. An idaya boy used to follow me when I went out to sell curds. I found out early enough that he had a roving eye! He used to try to chat me up and I would respond sourly! Once he was standing facing me, trying to flirt, when a huge bull attacked. It threw him in the air and kicked him over. I was stupefied with fear. I could not sleep for many days! Close my eyes, and I would see his intestines on the bull's horns . . . his teasing words were still in my ear . . .'

Her words made me shrink within.

'I know that his love was more than just playful banter. He told me that if he could not have me, he would wear a garland of the ash-coloured erikku flowers and set himself alight on a pyre by the wayside. He was making the wooden horse for it, he said. I may have been rude to him, but in my heart I never hated him . . .'

When the shadow of sorrow began to fall on her words and creep over them, she quickly changed her tone, as though to escape it: 'But there is something, you know, about us idaya women! We may fall in love, but we take as husbands only men who face a raging brute of a bull and overpower it in a straight fight . . .'

As if to prevent the hidden sorrow welling in her mind from spilling over into mine, I too laughed, deliberately.

We went past the idaya homes. Beyond them were some houses of the anthanar. We could hear some of them recite their holy verses. Those who did not know how to recite carved bangles from conch shells. Kiliyolam stopped in front of such a house.

'I really, really want some of these bangles!'

She took the lid off the pot and measured out the curds.

'After you bring us curds for two more days, you'll get four of these bangles,' the old man who took the curds from her assured her. Kiliyolam smiled.

I was thinking about the bullfight. If you are in love, why measure the body's prowess? To make a young girl watch that terrible sight – the sight of the youth who yearned for her battling monstrous bulls, dangling between life and death! What greater cruelty can one imagine?

Kiliyolam caught hold of my arm and we walked away. It was not the sweet notes of the flute, but the boom of the waves crashing on boulders by the seashore that fell on my ears. This girl who was so infatuated with conch-shell bangles must also be partial to the rumble of the waves.

We reached the market. Kiliyolam stopped at a shop in front of which hung many kinds of body ornaments. She shook a waist-chain of frog-mouth bells to check for its tinkle.

The shopkeeper smiled. 'Why do you want it?'

She shook her head to say no.

'You want it, don't you? What use do you have for it?'

It was for smaller children. Kiliyolam was an older child.

'It is for Taramma's girl. It is nice to see the darling little ones wear it.'

But I knew that she did not have any coin to pay for it. 'Let's get it another time.'

We turned to walk back home. I will get Taramma's little girl that chain, I vowed in my mind. But how? I did not have any coin either!

We now heard a tumult, somewhere in the distance. Kiliyolam made haste to return home.

'It's getting dark. That ruckus is probably by fellows drunk on ariyal. We'd better get home soon. Or we'll have to suffer their sweet nothings!'

That warning perked me up. Time flies if you hang out with this girl!

The sounds grew close quicker than we expected. It was not the kovalar; it was some soldiers riding up the path. My heart began to pound at just seeing them. Whose braided hair is going to fall prey to their swords now!

They were few in number. The red dust rising up from the horse hooves hitting the path clouded our sight. We blinked, rubbed our eyes and continued to walk. The cows, which ambled ahead swishing their tails, stirred the dust again before it could settle.

'Let's wait till the dust settles a bit,' I said, stopping by a tangle of jasmine vines on the wayside. 'Wonder if they are going to make war here too?'

Feeling the quiver in my tone, Kiliyolam placed her hand on my shoulder.

'Don't be afraid, Chithire . . . This is a high road, it leads to many places. The fighting may not be anywhere near. Troops pass by quite often.'

I was brushing the reddish dust off the white flowers with my fingers. Suddenly something poked my finger hard, and I pulled it away.

Kiliyolam pulled the tangled vines apart to check. She found cacti growing there, but still peered to make sure that there were no snakes. I felt no fear; I joined her. There was something shiny lying on the ground, in the red dust that had been brushed off the flowers.

A flower carved in gold!

I was astonished. I showed it to Kiliyolam.

'See this? A golden flower!'

She took it from me and examined it closely.

'This is not an ordinary flower. This is the gift of honour, the pookkol, which kings bestow on brave warriors in wars.'

'How did it get here? Maybe one of the warriors who passed by just now dropped it?'

'How to return this? The one who lost this is sure to return when he finds it missing. But we can't wait till then. It's already late!'

We kept walking ahead half-heartedly. We shouldn't have picked it up at all!

'Haven't you heard the story of the anklet with the beads of pearls inside? Yes, if it belongs to a king, we must be very afraid indeed!'

I had heard of it too. This pookkol too had a king's seal stamped on it. A shiver passed through my spine.

119

We were not mistaken. At a distance, a warrior had dismounted and was searching the sides of the road intently. The pookkol sat inside my hand, trembling.

The man's eyes were scanning the sides of the road. He neared us. When Kiliyolam clapped her hands to catch his attention, my very life seemed to stand still.

He inclined his head towards us. An unremarkable man with a strong body and an inscrutable face.

'What are you searching for?' Kiliyolam's voice faltered a little.

'I dropped something valuable that the king had bestowed on me,' he said. His voice did not match the hefty frame. He continued, probably because we were silent. 'It is made of gold. A pookkol.'

'We found it.'

His face brightened instantly at Kiliyolam's words.

Before he could say anything more, I held it out to him. He grabbed it in a second and looked up at me only after he had taken a good look at it.

'It's like I have got my life back! I don't know what to tell you!' His voice grew gentler.

Kiliyolam pulled my arm and began to walk briskly. I got ahead of her quickly.

'Please wait,' he called out to us. 'Tell me, what reward can I offer you?'

'Nothing! It's good that we are able to return to others things of value that belong to them! It is now with the rightful owner. We do not need anything more.'

It was I who spoke this time. My own words amazed me.

'You are good of heart. May the kindness of the gods and men and kings be always with you!'

He looked at me again. This time his face was brighter. He bowed to us respectfully.

I did not stay to answer. All I wanted then was to free myself from his gaze. I hurried, not even waiting for Kiliyolam. She caught up with me, running. When his horse sped past us, I covered my eyes again, fearing that the dust would rise up and choke us once more. He disappeared from sight. We got back home. His enigmatic gaze stayed locked in my sight – an irritating speck of dust in my eye.

Four

One evening, Perumpaanan summoned all of us. He began to speak without preface.

'I am just back from meeting the village headman. There's going to be a manchuvirattal here next week. They would like us to sing and dance.'

'What's a manchuvirattal?' asked Cheera, clearly puzzled.

Perumpaanan continued, 'It is a custom here, also a celebration, a kind of sport. They also call it eruthazuthal. Falling in love is not enough to win the hands of idaya maidens. The men must fight big bulls and make them yield. And they actually keep really angry beasts for the fight. Just seeing them stomping on the virattu field and panting hard makes you shake with fear!'

'So, what are we supposed to do?' Ulakan asked.

'We are to beat our drums and announce the manchuvirattal. And accompany the bullfights with our songs and drumming. After the bullfights, they will dance the kuravakkoothu; we have to join that too.'

No one uttered a word. Memories of the terrible things that had befallen us from dancing and singing were still fresh. The pain hung heavy in each and every heart.

'Do not ache from the sorrows of the past. Let them be the manure for our gains in the future.'

Perumpaanan's words did not bring back the light of hope into any face.

'We are skilled singers and dancers. That doesn't seem to matter here . . . We just do whatever, for whomever. Our dance and song seem to dissolve in the noise . . .'

'Is not our very life like that, Ulakaa?' asked Perumpaanan. 'Each grain of our lives falls in its moment, melts, disappears! Dance and music are born on the stage and they die there too. My child, what else is left of us but some faint sounds and slight shadows of body movement, even in the memory of those who try to recollect them?'

Ulakan was silent. One could see the dark shadows of selfishness in his words. And in Perumpaanan's words, the mellowness of a man who had seen much in life. So what, really? We knew well that our lives would need such tunings when we settled here. Maybe I felt that way because I live life day to day. I turned kind eyes towards Ulakan.

Preparations for the eruthazuthal were in full swing in the village. Men who coveted brides from the wealthy families of Koyikathillam, Pichkacheri and Mundakathilam were readying for the bullfight. Though Perumpaanan had told Ulakan to beat the drum and announce the event in the village, he did not budge. I think Perumpaanan still hurt from Achan's absence. His word was always the last word for Achan. Ulakan wasn't like that. Perumpaanan sent two others to make the announcements. They went from village to village announcing the names of the maidens ready to be married and calling forth young men who sought their hands to get ready for the manchuvirattal. A large arena and platforms were erected on wooden blocks on a vast ground. The decorated seats meant for the grandees and the village headman were set up around it. The bulls stood ready in their pens, their horns sharpened, waiting to tear into the fighting ring. Ulakan was going on and on about it, but it did not excite me.

The day of the manchuvirattal dawned. I went to the fighting ground with Perumpaanan and others.

Amma did not want to come. 'If you aren't going then I won't go,' said Cheera, and she stayed back. The way she withdrew into herself more and more these days pained me. For me, her presence in crowded places was no small relief.

We gathered our kuzhals and paras and found a place to sit near one of the raised arenas. The idayar men began to enter the ground wearing garlands of jasmine, pidavu, karunthu and venkaanthal flowers. The idayar maidens were dressed in garments of thazha and wore their hair in five braids bedecked with flowers of many hues. When they entered, the men cheered loudly. The women began to climb onto the platforms around the arena. I searched for Kiliyolam and Thaamara and Pachakkili in the crowd. They were not to be found.

The bulls were brought into the ground. Their keepers struggled to control them. The brute energy that had been contained while they were inside their pens seemed to gush out now. Each time a beast charged into the ring, the crowd bellowed. It felt like the panting of a thousand hunting dogs released together, all at once. I shrank inwardly, wondering what we were expected to do. Someone from the crowd turned towards us and raised their hand, and Perumpaanan's large cymbals let out their resounding metallic clang. Ulakan and I joined him. The bullfight had already enthralled Ulakan; he was in a state of high excitement. Our people began to beat the big drums and sound the kuzhals. The roll of the drums and the blare of the kuzhals wrestled with the roar of the crowd. The crowd's feverish passion was infecting the music. I looked at Ulakan. Just a little while ago, he had been preaching about the essence of music and dance, and now . . . I was taken aback.

Young idayar men prepared to grapple with the bulls in the arena. Some of them rubbed their hands together and punched the floor, trying to show their strength. The waves of fear that crashed and rolled through some of them showed in their eyes. But they suppressed the quiver in their bodies and joined the others. As they assembled, the idayar's aachaariyar invoked the blessings of the divine. They held up bamboo canisters filled with smouldering akil wood. Tendrils of smoke rose up into the air. Will the god of the idayar, who lives in lakes and tall trees, be merciful to these young men?

My heart filled with fondness when I saw the young idayar who were barely men; their cheeks were still round and childlike. Were the girls they loved seated on these platforms wringing their hands in sheer anxiety, melting inwardly bit by bit? How can women build courage in their men who struggled between love and death without letting their fear show? When the curls of akil fumes thickened and it became hard to see the waiting contestants, I immersed myself in the rasping sounds of the clashing cymbals.

'Sound the big drums!' The crowd yelled to us. Loud aarpu cheers and the sound of ululation filled the air. Drum beats that made both body and heart tremble began to climb towards a crescendo. The fight was starting. A massive white bull with curved, menacing horns drew itself up for a second like a bow ready to shoot and launched itself into the arena. Facing it was a young man with a broad chest and muscled shoulders, every nerve of his body alert.

In a split second, and against all expectation, the bull gored the man, twirled him once and tossed him in the air. The din from the spectators ceased suddenly. The very moment he hit the ground, the bull's horns plunged into his chest. I closed my eyes tight. But I could still see his life grind to a halt without him letting out even a single shriek of pain.

When I opened my eyes, I saw the crowd swaying in frenzy again. Two beasts had entered the fray now; two young men leapt in to take them on. I shuddered when it appeared that both the crowd and these men had totally forgotten, very quickly indeed, that one of them had been gored to death right in front of them! Even if just for a moment, I hated them – the crowd and Ulakan. The small bronze cymbals felt very heavy in my hands. My fingers refused to move. In the boom of the big drums, no one would have missed the humble minor cymbals.

The grappling continued in the arena. Many young men fought many animals. Human screams and animal grunts commingled; the roar of the crowd continued unabated. We kept drumming and blowing the bugles. The brief interludes of silence that punctuated the combats in the beginning disappeared now. The crowd cheered aloud when one of the combatants – man or beast – hit the ground. The corpses were removed, but their twisted and sundered limbs that lay scattered all over must have been hidden by the immense clouds of dust that had been kicked up. The clamour rose to its highest pitch, after which it could rise no more.

I woke up from my trance-like state when I felt Perumpaanan's hand on my shoulder. When I started to beat the cymbals again, he took them from me gently and handed them to someone else. I looked at the arena. The crowd was raising up the victors on their shoulders. Some of the idaya girls cheered them loudly. Some of them sat despondently on the platforms, heads bowed, drowning in tears. They must have had loved ones among both the young men who succumbed to death and those who faced it and returned. The cheering women climbed down into the arena. They clapped for us to join in; we climbed down from the platform and went to them.

It was time to get ready for the kuravakkoothu. We set aside the big drums and fetched our smaller drums and lutes. The idaya women began to sing; some of us accompanied them on our lutes. Then the idayar began to dance. We joined them, beating the small drums hitched on our waistbands. Men and women crowded together, their shoulders pressing against each other as they sang and danced.

Even though I pretended to join in, something held me back at the start. But when the singing and dancing became ardent, I could not help tumbling deep into it. The couples among the idayar moved away from the main group gradually to more secluded spots. I tried to avoid the press of the bodies. Chanthan was my partner in dance. The lack of that male body that filled the gaps between my steps and poses – it pressed close to me as yet another absence.

Then I realized that a firm hand was trying to pull me close and turned to look. It was the soldier – the one we had met on the road. His gaze was not like the one we had seen on his face when he got his pookkol back. He was dancing, and in between trying to clasp me closer to him. I shook him off, but he held on to my arm. Suddenly a terrible rush of hatred shot through my body. I freed my arm from his grip and ran. He seemed surprised for a moment. I dived into the crowd, looking for my people. But they too had scattered. The few who were still in the arena were joining the dance with their drums and lutes.

He did not come towards me again, but I felt like I was on dangerous terrain. Wanting badly to find a familiar face, I pushed through the dancers with difficulty. Taramma was standing at a distance with her child. I ran up to her and took the little one in my arms.

'Where is Kiliyolam? Did you see her?'

Taramma said something, but the din was so loud that I could not hear her, so she pointed to the distance. Kiliyolam, Thaamara and Pachakkili were standing there, together. They were dancing. They did not have partners – and that made me smile within. I went towards them, holding the child and coddling it.

They looked puzzled for a moment – probably because I had left my people behind and gone towards them. What? asked Kiliyolam, arching her eyebrows. I thought that she wouldn't hear even if I shouted, so I gestured with my eyes, pointing into the distance. He was nowhere to be seen; she did not understand what I was trying to say. But she made some space for me between them and held me close. That was enough for me to feel that I was among loved ones. Humble acts of care, to ease small fears. Little acts of kindness, revealed in a look or a hug. Their value is sometimes simply inestimable, I felt. I saw that there was something special in the friendship of women, something that a male protector could never give.

After some time, Taramma too joined us. I had told Kiliyolam all that had happened by then. The singing and dancing continued, even though it was getting late. But we did not stay; we returned before evening fell. I was afraid that he might follow us. As if they knew it, the idaya girls accompanied me to my doorstep. In the end when they too left, dusk, neither dark nor light, kept me company.

Five

I did not go out at all for some days. Feeling rather out of sorts, I stayed at home with Cheera and Amma. Kiliyolam would drop in when she went out to sell curds. I just did not feel like accompanying her. I wanted to stay with Cheera. She sat on our veranda, her hair dishevelled, looking like a peacock that had not yet learned to dance. Her inner world was even less decipherable these days. She sought not the harmony of the things that existed in the real world but the unknown paths deep in her mind. And stubbornly refused to share her wanderings. Sitting beside her, I thought – this girl is like an idol of stone that bears in its heart the traces of many past births.

'What's on your mind?'

I had to break the silence that was growing between us.

She was quiet for a few moments, and then began to speak. Her voice was as gentle as the breeze brushing against leaves.

'I had a terrible dream last night. Of another world – but rather like ours. Achan and Annan were there with the rest of us. And this dream world had everything that our world doesn't have. Also, it had all the things that were gone from this world. It was as if this dream world completed ours! It had clear skies, a cold, frozen sea and an unmoving forest. On the still waves of the frozen sea, our little children were playing a game of tag. I went out to join them, but Achan stopped me. Then some argument broke out between Annan, whom I have never seen before, and Achan, who held me by the hand. And a bunch of people rushed at us . . .'

She paused a moment. Her words trembled when she spoke again.

'Suddenly the skies turned an angry red. The waves began to roll. The trees in the forest began to sway and shake. The waters in the sea began to boil; the trees caught fire. The shadows of living men who were crouching under the trees in fear now leapt up. They were running away, afraid that the fire raging in the dried deadwood might swallow them whole! The searing wind blew hard, spitting angrily, uprooting the trees. The deer, their bodies half-eaten by the flames, thrashed about in agony trying to free their antlers which were caught in the thorn bushes that the blaze had torn apart . . .'

Feeling hot tears prick my eyes, I clapped my palm on her mouth: say no more, I silently begged. She fell silent. She stayed that way even after I pulled my hand away.

Then, after some time, she continued, 'I can still see it . . . the charred thickets of cane . . . the clumps of bamboo, still smouldering . . . burned pieces of bone, scattered everywhere. The stench of burned flesh, filling every corner . . .'

Her words kept flowing; I got up and went looking for Amma. She was sleeping on the bare floor. Her eyeballs thrashed about under her closed eyelids; they made little waves under them. Amma must have heard us. Or she must be writhing inwardly from her own nightmares.

Let her sleep, I thought. I did not feel like sitting beside Cheera either, so I stepped out of the house and went to our backyard. The mass of greenery behind the row of kanchi trees rose and fell. The meadow looked like a young girl stretched out in slumber, her head resting on her arm. As I stood there watching it, something moved in the distance. It was either cows or deer, but soon it was clear that a girl walked beside them – and that it was Kiliyolam. I saw her cross into the meadow past the row of trees and hailed her, but she did not hear me.

A light breeze blew. The grasses were flirting with it. I did not want to stomp on the karuka grass and press down their playful blades, so I walked carefully, stepping on the small islands of reddish soil between the patches of grass.

If only I could stop myself from hurting another, even with the pressure of my feet on the ground! If only I could walk beside all life in the world caressing it like a gentle shade! I yearned to be like that, in vain.

Suddenly I heard those hoof beats that had made me shudder in fear! My dread, now in the shape of a living man, approached. It was him. The soldier.

My legs froze. I was all alone. I tried to call aloud Kiliyolam's name – she could be seen, ahead – but not even a low grunt would leave my throat. I felt dizzy; I feared that I might fall.

The soldier was very near now. There was no place to run to. My body was trembling. It had broken into a sweat.

He dismounted quickly and came up to me. When I saw him face to face, he appeared forlorn. He did not move. That surprised me, but I stayed alert, as I did not know what his intention was.

'Forgive me,' he said directly, folding his palms together. My only thought was to find a way to escape, somehow. I did not reply.

'When I saw you by the wayside that day, I just felt very grateful to you … for giving me back something so precious. I kept thinking of you. Seeing you among the drummers at the manchuvirattal surprised me for a moment. I was intrigued when I saw you join in a rather half-hearted way. Somehow, I felt close to you. That thing during the koothu . . . I didn't come near you on purpose . . .'

'What exactly do you want now?'

I was still shivering within, but my voice sounded quite harsh: good.

'Nothing . . .' He cleared his throat as if to say something, then decided against it and walked back towards his horse. He turned towards me again for a brief moment. 'It's not wrong for women and men to dance the kuravakkoothu together. I was just trying to tell you of the love I felt for you . . .'

'You did not try to find out if I felt the same love, did you? It is wrong that you tried to embrace me without knowing how I felt. That is not how you reveal your heart.'

'That is why I begged forgiveness. It was a momentary slip . . . it will never occur again, I promise. But let me tell you this: I hold within my heart nothing but love for you.'

I did not answer him. The fear and loathing I felt within had not subsided yet. He climbed back on the horse and cantered away.

I wearily turned around to go home. Kiliyolam had spotted me; she was clapping her hands, trying to call me. She soon caught up with me.

'What did he say?'

I told her everything, every detail. Something seemed to be clouding her mind. I asked her about it, but she just dismissed it. Then she came up to me and held my hand. 'He seems harmless, Chithire.'

I turned sharply to her — what had happened to this girl, I wondered.

She continued, rather reluctantly, 'I don't see you these days, that is why I did not tell you. I met this man again. He came over and spoke with me once. All his talk was about you. He is from Thakadur. His name is Makeeran.'

'What can he possibly say about me?'

'You know well what he feels for you. I told him that what he did to you without finding out about your feelings was wrong. He knows it too.'

I was suddenly overcome by strange misgivings. I went back home quickly without lingering to clarify my feelings.

'You are alone now. You need a man's love!'

Kiliyolam's voice reached me from behind. All I knew was that a shadow had been cast, both on my body and on the inner recesses of my mind. Anyway, what was there to think at length about love? Nothing beyond the inexplicable attraction of body to body, heart to heart! But I had no such feelings for this man — I could see that clearly. Had love completely vacated my heart? Or, was it that it had never existed in me? Or maybe it was in my inner world and I did not know it?

I did not feel like staying at home. Perumpaanan, Ulakan and some others were away in some neighbouring village. Ulakan did not like to go singing from house to house, hamlet to hamlet. But he probably relented, not wanting to defy Perumpaanan too many times. I was summoned only when many people were needed. That was probably because Perumpaanan knew that Amma and Cheera were still grieving. Yet when I stayed at home, home felt far away, outside me. Even if I coaxed myself to step out, I still felt tightly wound up within. I was neither in nor out of home. My inner world was not dark, but it was not filled with light either. A terrible lassitude had taken over.

In the evening, I ventured out to Kiliyolam's house. She was not at home, so I waited at Taramma's house, playing with her little daughter. Kiliyolam lifted up her arms when she saw me. I laughed aloud, seeing four conch-shell bangles on her arms, two on each. She seemed to have something to say, and so when she went out of the house, I followed her.

'Makeeran is still around. He comes over to talk when he sees me. Keeps asking about you. Maybe he feels that you hate him.'

I did not reply but I felt a tiny sliver of light fall on the pall of gloom that had shrouded me.

'Ah! That is a relief!' said Kiliyolam. 'Now I am wondering why he didn't have any such feelings for *me*! He saw us both that evening, didn't he?' she winked and laughed. And then, trying to bring back seriousness into her tone, she continued: 'Chithire, I know that you are rather glum these days. Why carry on here like this, neither here nor there? Makeeran does not seem ordinary for sure – he's won a pookkol from the king, after all. And I don't think his feelings for you are shallow. Only that I didn't want to tell you before I knew your mind. He's been asking me how he could meet you. What should I tell him?'

Kiliyolam was very close to me. She knew me well. I still hesitated.

'Your arms look so beautiful with those conch-shell bangles!' I tried to distract her. 'Nothing can match the striking combination of black and white!'

Kiliyolam began to look a little offended. 'I won't say a word! Never!'

'Hey, don't be angry, my girl! Actually, I don't know what to do or say. Let me go now. Let's meet later.'

Walking back home, I thought about the places from where the warmth welled up. More than Makeeran's love, it was Kiliyolam's care that touched me. The fear and disgust I felt towards Makeeran had vanished. But I was puzzled that his words had found no resonance at all in me. Was it because I knew nothing of love? Perhaps.

The house looked gloomier when I returned. Had dusk fallen earlier than usual? I did not want any supper. No one asked me, either. I went to bed early but could not sleep. My inner spaces had known nothing but music and dance. Were they now preparing for war? What was that red that flooded my eyes when I closed them? The colour of the chenkanthal flower, or blood? I could not make out.

I remember dozing off for a little while. It must have been around midnight; a horse's neigh rose from beyond the kanchi trees behind our house. Must be the rabbits scampering on the dry leaves, I told myself. Anyway, I did not get up or look out through the window.

When Kiliyolam came over the next morning, I told her this.

'It must have been him!' She sounded sure. I had a feeling that she was hiding something.

'I didn't tell you because I thought it would irk you. He knows where you live. He also told me that he lingers behind your house at night, when he rides this way. Chithire, it's just that he does not know how to show his love for you. I don't think he is the cruel sort. He's a soldier, isn't he? Soldiers must be mostly used to being a little rough.'

Then, on another night, when I heard something move outside the house, I did go out. He was waiting; it was as though he knew that I would go to him. He came closer. My heart did not pound harder. I felt neither fear nor shame. My body and spirit were numb, even in the delicate and cool night air in which the darkness and moonlight lay tenderly commingled.

I even felt that the I who stood beside him and the I who was inside me were different people altogether. I seemed to stand at a distance, watching him and me.

Neither of us spoke a word.

Maybe I had succumbed to his love to escape my world-weary, lonely existence.

'Don't you have anything to say?'

I said nothing. When his hand reached towards my shoulder, I flinched. He was taken aback for a moment. He stood there quietly, looking at me for some time. And then, slowly, he turned and began to walk away.

Suddenly, the thought that he might go away forever shot through me like a bolt of lightning.

'Please stay . . . for a moment?'

He stopped. I went up and took his rough hand. How did I warm to those fingers which had tried to draw my body forcibly, clumsily, towards him? How did I take to them, when their touch had made me once wince and curl up inwardly, like a millipede? There was no time to sift through my memories and recollect. He drew me closer, gently. A drop of defiance took shape in my mind, but it did not have the momentum to grow into resistance. He kissed me on the forehead and said, 'I cannot bear to see you in pain. Aren't you all alone? I too am alone. Is it not true that the divine spirit of love abides wherever lonesome ones unite?'

I did not feel like probing his words, their truth. When he caressed my head, something inside me eased itself into the gentle warmth of his fingers. We stayed under the kanchi trees till birdsong announced the coming of dawn. He freed himself from my hands, separated his body from mine, and got up. His horse was tethered a short distance away. He mounted it and galloped away through the highs and lows of the meadow. I felt as though some part of me was falling off. I saw before me the vast and verdant wild from which the gloom of the night had not yet withdrawn. The shadowy form of the horse and its rider rose and fell on the waves of lush green. Though the sight grew further and further away and finally disappeared, it lingered in my eyes.

Six

We met again and again in the meadow during the daytime and under the kanchi tree at night. One night, when the moonlight and the scent of jasmine blooms filled the air, he took my hand and we walked towards the meadow together. Makeeran pointed to the murky darkness of the jungle beyond the expanse of grass.

'Our king's camp is on the hill on the other side of that forest,' he said.

'Camp? What are you here for?'

'I cannot tell you, Chithire! There are things between those who rule the land that no one else can know. But this I can say – our king has been facing trouble from some of his rivals. There's a troop of soldiers around here now. He's come in person to prepare them for combat.'

So kings leave their palaces and live incognito – that was new knowledge for me.

'The camp is surrounded by thorn fences. Elephants are on guard near the main entrance. There are really good minders, from another land, to care for them.'

'It's not hard to finish off a king even inside his own abode. I have known that directly. What is the point of trying to guard him when he is outside?'

'You learned it directly? How?'

I told him of all the winding paths my people and I had traversed. He listened sympathetically, patting my back sometimes, or holding me close. I stopped when I reached the brink of tears, taking care not to fall into that chasm of pain.

'Enough of my story . . . what about the king's security? Tell me?'

I gathered myself and prepared to listen to him.

'This is only for your ears . . . The king stays in a special room inside the tent. It is camouflaged really well – arrows are fixed on the frame above it all around and cloth is flung on top, held up by the tips of the arrows. Inside the room, the king's guard is a troop of beautiful women who hide sharp little knives in their breast bands. It's not so easy to finish him off!'

He paused. I did not care to know more but pretended to pay attention.

'Their arms with the bangles jingling on them ... are so tempting in the soft light of the oil lamps . . .'

He threw me a sly look. It was easy for me to feign envy.

My thoughts were about the soldiers' camp. I did not even know where Makeeran lived! Reading my mind, he said, 'We live in huts inside the forest. We took over the homes of the nayadis. During the day we cut down trees and chip away at the boulders to clear a path for the battle . . .'

I felt no desire at all to learn more about the king or his war. When he mentioned the nayadis who had lost their homes, I remembered the aiynar who had given us refuge . . .

'Doesn't the king need many soldiers?'

'The other rooms of the tent are full of soldiers. The walls are mounted with many spears. Do you know? We even have yavana soldiers fighting with us!'

'Yavana?'

'Yes. They come from afar, from across the sea. Their skin is of a different colour. We can't make out their language. They dress differently – their breast-plates and headdresses are distinct. They wear long shirts and belts of leather. Just their piercing stares are enough to make you afraid! All is fair for them in battle … they will try any trick to win! The king also has guards from the northern places, far off …'

We had walked some distance through the grass by then.

A sudden terror gripped me. This man is a stranger, I felt, and I was being led through an unfamiliar land the words and ways of which were unknown to me.

'Let's go back.'

'What's this, Chithire? Aren't you ready to be with me even now?'

I had already turned back. His hand fell on my shoulder and I stopped.

'I came here only to search for you … that was the only reason.'

Makeeran was speaking the truth. I came to know of that only much later. At that moment, it sounded like a common way of describing the enduring bonds of past births or the ties that bind lovers in this birth. That is probably why it brought tears to my eyes. I fervently wished that the hands that had stroked my back so tenderly, that had held me with so much warmth, would never let go. When I raised my head, he kissed me on my lips. Our bodies pressed the closest they could to each other. I did not feel like stopping the lips that fell on my cheeks and neck, and the hand which fondled my breasts. The buds of the venkanthal, which look like fingers joined on a hand, were falling all over my body …

I reached home only when day was about to break.

It was during one of those days that Chanthan returned. Annan was not with him. To all those who asked him about Mayilan, he offered nothing but a pained silence. When he came to our house, he stayed outside, probably because of his reluctance to meet Amma. But she came out to meet him anyway, as though the long wait had been only, and only, for this meeting.

'You didn't find him, did you? My child! All this wandering of yours, futile! You should not have gone seeking . . . I know so well that this life offers nothing but loss . . . But then, you are back safe . . . that is good enough.'

Chanthan stood silent, his head bowed.

'Is he alive? Could you find out at least that?'

'Yes, only that. I don't know where he is.'

'Ah, at least we know that he is alive. Good! You took our pain on your shoulders, of your own accord. I gave birth to him, but maybe it was wrong to have longed to have him back when you were with us.'

Chanthan's eyes welled up. To hide it, he smiled. But his natural charm and liveliness seemed to have vanished.

'How did you find out that we are here?' I asked, not wanting to sadden him further.

'I covered the whole of the route that you took. Before that, I covered Mayilan's route – but I could not go all the way.'

All our people had gathered by then. Chanthan must have thought that this was a good moment to share everything.

'I went to Ezhimala. I reached the place in three or four days. People there had begun to forget Nannan's death, but the shattered fortresses and filled-up moats were still there. I was in a fix, because it was not possible to find out anything about the king or Mayilan. Remember what Paranar told us? There are things there which we don't know about! I finally learned something when I met an old man who used to serve at the king's palace. I don't know if all that he said about Mayilan is true. He didn't go there to be a singer. He began as a gardener but did not work in the garden for long. Apparently, more than war, he was interested in palace intrigues! It looks like he was quite close to the king. When the king went into hiding, unable to face the might of the Chera, he too went with him. No one knows where.'

Amma went back in.

Ulakan asked what all of us had wanted to ask ever since we heard him mention Annan. 'Back in Parambumala, Achan kept saying that a man we saw there – called Chami – was Annan. Can we find out if he and Annan are the same?'

'When I could not find Mayilan, I went to Parambumala,' said Chanthan. 'You were supposed to be there, so I thought I could join you there. There, I got to know about everything that had happened and decided to look for you. I don't know anything about Chami.'

'How did you find out that we are here, son?'

Perumpaanan broke his silence only then.

'I was told that you were escorted to the border by guards. The people there are totally shaken by their king's murder. They don't know whom to trust, how to tell apart friend from foe. They don't think well of us, either . . . so I did not stay there for long. I went to the border and guessed where you were likely to go. And when I reached this place, some folk told me about the paanars who had danced and drummed at the eruthazuthal. That must be my people, I reckoned. Then it was easy to find you.'

Though he could not find Annan, Chanthan's return made everyone feel as though a paralysed limb in our body had revived. Annan, who had left the flock early, was an absence for most of us. A memory that receded further the more we searched for him. But Chanthan was different. He had left a little – as sight and sound and touch – in each of us before he went away. Maybe some of that which was lost in his absence could be retrieved now. Maybe his return was a new beginning.

All this while, I was in another land. In the land of those who wore armour but hid away instead of fighting. The two of us, Makeeran and I, in my mind, were in a tent in the middle of a camp covered with many-coloured cloths and with leafy little huts. Sometimes that land faded when regular sights crowded my eye. In such moments, I would gaze at the waves of green that played in the meadow. The scent of another, which had now become part of my body, ended my loneliness. I felt a new tenderness towards the world. I forgave all those who had hurt me.

'Now you are smiling all the time!'

Kiliyolam threw that at me playfully; I smiled. But her eyes moistened.

'I knew what you needed. You really like him, don't you?'

I had not really thought much about that. But I wanted Makeeran to be with me all the time. My gaze sped ahead through the gap between the kanchi trees time and again. Makeeran came to meet me again through the path cleared by my gaze. Our love seemed to bloom in the blue kaya flowers, the golden clusters of the konna tree, the white kodal buds and the red kanthal blossoms.

Makeeran lay on my lap. He stroked my flowing locks of hair that fell around his face. He caressed my breasts. The night passed quickly. I was returning home before dawn broke when I noticed a shadow disappearing quickly into a clump of trees. I stopped in my tracks, suddenly alert.

'Who's that?'

I don't know if my voice came out, but the form stepped out of the shade of the trees.

It was Chanthan. I could not utter a word. He cleared his throat to say something, but said nothing. He turned and walked away briskly.

I did not see him anywhere during the day. I feared that he might come again when I went out at night, but that did not happen. A couple of days passed thus. Somehow, I felt drained, without energy. What would have Chanthan thought? Then, one evening, when I was returning after meeting Kiliyolam, I ran into him. I winced a little, but did not try to evade him. He seemed reluctant to walk beside me; he just stood there.

When I resumed my walking, he called me: 'Chithire, who is he?'

'A soldier.'

I told him all that I could tell about Makeeran. But Chanthan's face did not light up.

'I find it hard to say anything, Chithire,' he finally said. 'I'm in a hurry now. You can go.'

'That won't do,' I told him. 'Let's walk together. Whatever you feel, you must tell me.'

'You have made your decision. I am too late.'

I was a little unnerved. I knew his heart. He never told me of it, but always offered such tender care. But speaking affectionately to him would be wrong,

I thought, and held myself back. Speaking thus would be to betray Makeeran.

Abruptly, Chanthan turned around and walked away. I stood there. Then in a sudden burst of courage, I called out to him: 'Please wait?'

My voice sounded more serious than I wanted it to be.

'It's not enough to be brave outside. You need to be brave from within, too. It is true that I did catch a flash now and then of what was on your mind. But it was never really revealed. And when you went away, there was no way to find out, either.'

'I revealed my heart through what I did. I went away searching for your brother. And all of us set out in search of the means to rid ourselves of want. I wanted all our sorrows to end. I wanted us to live together for the rest of our lives. That's why I returned so quickly, sought you out . . .'

My heart felt impossibly heavy. Chanthan was a good man. He had no one in the world. I knew well how much affection my parents had for him, and how much he loved them in return. But it did not bring tears to my eyes. The depth of my love for Makeeran was also revealed to me. My heart beat hard when it struck me that love towards one could be cruelty towards another. I walked away as fast as I could, without another look at Chanthan.

Seven

It was a moonlit night in which the shade of the vila trees fell upon the blue flowers of the kaayaavu that blossomed just once a year. When we were about to part, Makeeran said, 'It is almost time for the troop to return. It looks certain that there will be no battles any time soon.'

Makeeran did not sound sad or disturbed. He was reaching up to pluck a bunch of flowers.

'"Troop"? Shouldn't you be saying "us"?'

'Yes, "us" it should be. No doubt about that! But will you be able to come with me?'

'How will I be able to not come?'

'I do want you to come. But we can't leave now. I will go now and return soon. Then let us set out together.'

I felt drained. As though everything that I had built up in my mind had suddenly collapsed. I gripped his hand hard to steady myself. We both sat leaning on a tree.

'I will die if you don't return . . .'

Makeeran held me close. The night was now caught in a warp of pain. It broke into pieces.

Makeeran left. I knew that he would be back soon to take me with him. But it was not easy to pass the time.

One day, when Perumpaanan and others were about to go to some neighbouring place or the other,

Chanthan's steely voice rose: 'Did we march all this way here for this? If it was only to be dancing and singing in somebody's homestead then we should have never left our place.'

Before Perumpaanan could say anything, Ulakan joined Chanthan. 'I have been saying this for long. Why do we waste our lives like this?'

No one responded, so I had to speak up.

'We have lived our lives in these ways till now, haven't we? What reason do we have to change it now?'

Chanthan threw me a grim look.

'Whatever – I don't want to live like this. I couldn't find Mayilan. But we need to escape this endless needy existence. We must go find a patron, a king.'

I was rather surprised to see that Perumpaanan did not disagree with him.

'If so, where should we go to?'

It seemed that everyone was ready to set off for a new land. Chanthan must have told the others about my entanglement. I worried that a decision might be reached before I could intervene.

'Why are you hurrying so?'

I felt my voice growing faint, and so tried to harden my tone.

'I can't leave this place now!'

'Oh, we know why!' Ulakan raised his voice.

'Yes. What you know is true. I am not willing to leave this place now. I have to stay back here.'

'Chithire . . .' Perumpaanan turned to me, but did not complete his sentence. Instead, he addressed the others.

'Isn't she our child? Don't desert her. If she is not coming, I am not coming either.'

My eyes filled with tears; I turned abruptly and strode back into the house. It seemed rather quiet outside. After some time, Perumpaanan came in.

'Everyone seems determined to leave . . . I know why. My daughter, you are capable of sifting the good from the bad. No one is going to leave without knowing your mind. And you too will have to take some decisions now.'

'What is there to decide now? Shouldn't I wait till Makeeran returns? It's my failing that I did not tell anyone of it. I just thought that you'd be with me when you came to know. Now . . .'

I could not complete what I wanted to say. I finished my sentence in another way.

'Have you decided where you are going?'

'To the land of the Chera, everyone says. Chanthan says that Kapilar went there.'

'To the land of the Chera who killed Paari? Are the daughters of Vel Paari still with him? Are they married now? If it was the Mighty Three that slew Paari by stealth, would Kapilar seek refuge with one of them? And even if he does, would Paari's daughters go with him?'

I found it all incomprehensible.

An ironic smile appeared on Perumpaanan's face. 'That does not matter to us. Don't you remember what Paranar said? Kings need applause and poets sing their praises. It can be the other way too. The paanar need coin; they need a king to gift it to them. If not this king, then another, that is all! Aren't we hurrying now to seek refuge with the Chera who abandoned our ancestors? Ah! Let that be! It is Paari's daughters who've lost the most. Kapilar took them along as he went from chieftain to chieftain, begging them to take the innocent girls in. But all of them refused – they were too afraid of the Mighty Three, people say. In the end he had to entrust them to the anthanar who live at Thirukkoviloor.'

'If this is how it is, who can we trust? The road to palaces may be broad, but the corridors within them are narrow. It is not easy to know the minds of kings and those who surround them, is it?'

What if Makeeran does not return?

A sudden terror gripped me.

'We will leave only after he comes back. I will not let anyone go till then.'

Perumpaanan went away. I felt many different thorns pierce my heart, all at the same time. I already knew how deep the pain would be in the coming days; only that I did not know how to overcome it.

On sleepless nights I lay in bed alert for the sound of horse's hooves. I started up from sleep at the rustling of leaves. In the moonlight, the shadows of the kanchi trees were a murky black. Beyond it, darkness hung heavy above the meadow.

Four or five days passed thus. I wanted to spend more time with Amma, but I could not. Too many thoughts crowded within. I went to meet Kiliyolam and Thaamara, and I played with Taramma's little one. I knew nothing of the future except that I would leave them all.

I did not wait in vain. Early one morning, Makeeran returned. The wind, playful above the green glory of the meadow. Bird-call from the canopies of the kanchi trees. The spirited dance of life filling the world. I had been rocking between life and death – that painful swaying ended. I took many deep breaths. I embraced him hard and wept.

'So we can go now, can't we?' Not knowing where my heart stood, I mumbled.

My heart had become infirm. I had become so ready to part from my own folk! Makeeran stroked my hair.

'Shouldn't we tell your Amma? Will your people let you leave with me if they come to know?'

I told him all that had happened. They knew everything. There was nothing left to decide. Suddenly, I wanted to see Amma and Perumpaanan. I was leaving all my loved ones. A shaft of lightning that tore apart the dark and heavy rain clouds passed through my body. My spirit was splintering. Makeeran held me close and we walked towards my home. I wiped my eyes.

Amma was near the doorway. I took a step back, a little hesitant. She did not move. But I could see tender shoots of kindness in her eyes.

'So you are leaving too, aren't you? Ah, you have to! Your man looks like a good spirit. And you will not bring him pain, I know. To live together is a virtue! Only good will happen to you.' She blessed us.

Perumpaanan too said the same. All my people gathered around us. They were in a hurry to depart. Ulakan seemed to be immersed in packing. Were they just waiting to get rid of me? Maybe not. They too must be preoccupied about their future; I was not alone in that.

They are going to Muchiri. Chanthan had apparently found out that the Chera king had been staying there for some time now. A big town. A place where they get coin from merchants from far, for things that we make here. Many there are now rich, earning a lot of paddy for fish. They want to meet the king. Till then, they will survive. There are many rich folk there, after all.

The threads of affection that bound me to my people were breaking one by one. Coin is above love, so it seemed. If it were not so, would they have been in such a hurry to leave, without a care about my lot? There was nothing left to do but bid goodbye.

When I got out of the house, I bent down and scooped up a handful of soil in my hand. I held it tightly. This soil had offered us refuge. It smelled of both blood and milk.

I remembered Kiliyolam and Thaamara and Pachakkili. And the lovely smile on Taramma's little girl's face. I must meet them once more when we leave.

Makeeran mounted his horse and held his arm out to me. I could only shrink away; then he lifted me up easily as though I were as light as a bundle of cotton. His rough hands tightened their grip as he raised me up; it hurt. Seated on the horse and held between his arms, I forgot all fear and pain. I did not even feel the horse racing ahead. It stopped when we reached the homes of the idayar. The doors were shut. Though we called out many times, no one answered. And then we left. As we sped ahead on the reddish paths, I stowed away in my heart a toddler's smile and the faint, receding scent of milk. Those would be the salves of my spirit.

Eight

The horse galloped so fast; it almost flew. Makeeran had me firmly in the crook of his left arm, like a bird that was being snatched away. Many times in my life,

I have wanted to fly. I imagined flying to be a release from the very world. But when I sat on Makeeran's horse in his secure embrace, it was as though a bird was rising, nest and all. I leaned on him and stroked his forearm. His lips pressed on the back of my neck now and then through my wind-tossed hair; they were warm and wet. Even as I tried to stop his hand from wandering on my breasts, deep inside I kept yearning for their touch. Those rude hands which I once disliked so much were now my sole refuge in the world – the thought brought tears to my eyes. I closed them.

Humid air rose up from the undulating meadows on either side of the path. Frolicking fawns ran away at the sound of our approach. The rows of kanchi trees on the wayside ran backwards and disappeared from sight without lingering in the eye, like memories of paths once trodden. A peacock slipped down to the ground from the bough of a mango tree that leaned down towards the road. We did not feel like stopping anywhere. We wanted to sprint ahead, disappear into the distance. In my heart, waves lapped on the lonely seashore and left it wet.

It was getting dark, but the heat kept growing. At first, I did not notice the greenery receding. Now it was almost gone. The dry road too was changing colour. The horse's hooves clattered on the craggy and broken rocks. The horse began to slow down.

'The sandy wastes are ahead of us. We can't go this way at night,' said Makeeran.

I felt a cold gust of terror. A sandy stretch, completely deserted. Blackened tree branches, scorched by the unrelenting summer. The skeletons of dead animals. The maravar, bandits who hid by the wayside to pounce on travellers, would not spare even the poor. Many sights – some that I had already seen, some which were to come – flashed through my mind.

'What will we do now?'

My trembling voice made Makeeran burst out laughing.

'You need not be afraid. No one will dare to touch Makeeran and his woman.'

The horse made its way through the dark warily. It stopped, panting, after steep climbs. I too gasped, as though I had taken its weariness into myself. Neither Makeeran's kisses nor his playful hand on my breasts could soothe me. The caked darkness that surrounded us was seeping into my spirit.

Suddenly some people leapt in front of us, brandishing lit torches and yelling. I shuddered. The horse could not move. I felt the tip of a spear on the hollow of my neck and froze; I could not even scream.

'It's me, Makeeran,' he called out, pushing away the spear-tip at my throat with his sword. The strident sounds that had hurtled down at us suddenly ceased. They recognized him by his voice before the light of their torches fell on him.

He helped me get down and then dismounted. They were all staring at me now. I shrank when some of them advanced towards us.

'She is my woman.'

Those who came towards us stepped back. Some exchanged sly looks through the corners of their eyes and grinned.

'Don't have to ask if it's stolen or truly given! It's Makeeran, after all . . .' someone sniggered.

Makeeran did not like it. 'Not stolen,' he cut in. 'Her people know. I brought her along with their knowledge.'

I was still troubled. Probably sensing my unease, Makeeran got in front of me.

'We are spending the night here, we will leave tomorrow.'

He said that to them, but it was my mind that got scalded. These were maravar, who looted for a living. Ruthless, devoid of kindness. Spend a night with such people? But I could not speak a word.

'Don't be afraid,' Makeeran reassured me. 'Not one of these fellows will lay a finger on us.'

We walked behind them. Jagged stones bit our feet. The light of the torches grew dim when it reached the ground.

We reached a small single-room cloth tent. A lit clay lamp stood beside the mat laid on the ground. My fear did not abate, though we were alone now.

'Aren't these people robbers? Why are they not trying to rob us?'

'Today is our first night together. Don't we have a lifetime to talk about other things?'

Makeeran embraced me. He caressed my curls gently. I was too nervous to even look up. One of his rugged hands fondled my breasts; the other stroked my back. He raised my chin and whispered in my ear: 'I am a man who walks at night. Your eyes overflow with moonlight. I was in search of your light. I can never free myself from the glow of your eyes . . .'

I closed my eyes. We sank down together onto the ground slowly. The lamp wick was lowered. On my eyelashes, the gentle pressure of his lips. My chest heaved and tautened. When his lips pressed on my breasts, I was filled with yearning: I let my nerves yield. My passion and tenderness yearned to brim over. Makeeran picked up the clay lamp and held it up against me. When I saw my body glint like a sword drawn from its scabbard, I could not help feeling a stab of pride. Feeling my whole body sweetly scarred by my man's pointed gaze, desire teeming in it, I shut my eyes. All over my body, thronging, swarming bees. They settled wherever it was soft and moist. My nerves twisted and knotted. Flashes of pain in between did not feel like pain. All the springs that rose from me flowed towards him. My eyes overflowed. I held back with my lips the moans that rose from my throat. When his heavy body pressed against mine, I held it tight. Then, I felt light. I slept off in the lightness of having set free all that was within me.

A sharp, piercing pain in my breast jolted me awake – it felt as though the blade of a chisel had sliced it. The reek of a body that I did not know assailed me. *This is not Makeeran,* I screamed in utter shock, shoving him off me and rolling to the other edge of the mat, snatching up my garments to cover myself. Makeeran too had woken up. Even in the darkness, I could see a man fall and writhe on the floor.

The lamp wick was raised again. Makeeran was plunging his knife into a still-struggling body. Blood spurted from the man's chest. A grunt, and then he was motionless. Makeeran pressed his foot down on the fallen body. I went up and leaned on him.

It took us some time to steady ourselves.

'Don't be scared. It was a maravan. Such things are common here. Anyone reckless enough to touch Makeeran's bride is a dead man.'

I shuddered again and again. Each time, a thorn was driven into my heart. This was becoming so familiar now. I no longer felt the pain as I once used to. Would this body of mine turn into a shirt of coarse cloth, rough and unfeeling, inside and out?

Makeeran lifted the bleeding man and threw him out of the tent. And then he said, as though nothing had happened: 'Come, let us go back to bed.'

I could not sleep. I managed to stay inside the tent somehow till it was daybreak. Makeeran kept drinking from a pot in a corner of the tent till it was empty.

I hurried to leave when it was dawn. Makeeran did not speak. He went towards his horse. It forgot all fatigue and got to its feet. Makeeran mounted it, lifted me up on it, and then called out aloud to the maravars: 'We are leaving! There's a corpse lying here. Bury it.'

No one responded. Not waiting for a reply, Makeeran spurred his horse.

The sandy wilderness stretched ahead. The highs and lows on the path were rocky. On the wayside, now and then, dried-up and dead trees. The sun had barely come up, but it was already scorching hot. Here and there, skeletons of dead cattle. But the drought within was worse. The greenery was vanishing bit by bit. Who is Makeeran? Soldier or bandit? The needle of a terrible fear pierced through my nerves, sewing them together. He was not opening up, in the least. Was something roaring and crashing like waves inside him as the horse galloped? His outward stillness scared me.

The harsh fields of sunlight in the sandy wild did not last very long. The green began to show again and it put out the coals smouldering in my mind.

We stopped at a large pond by the wayside. Cool water on my body made me feel alive again. The horse regained its vigour, feasting on the grass that grew beside the pond. We drank the clear water to our heart's content and rested for a while under a tree. I lay down, my head on Makeeran's lap. I did not want to get up. That I was able to relax under the shade of a thicket knotted up by thorny bushes and vines left me feeling amazed.

Makeeran was stroking my hair gently, but I could feel the urgency in his fingers. I could not rest much. We got back on the horse.

By noon, we neared a long range of hills. Pointing to one of the hills, Makeeran said, 'Kuthiramala.'

The horse did not seem to tire as we climbed the hill, only that it slowed down somewhat. It moved forward by the side of a couple of hills, half-running, half-walking. We reached the summit of Kuthiramala and then descended. The climb down and the flat expanse below made the horse livelier. I shut my eyes when the wind blew hard; then I leaned on Makeeran's chest and dozed off.

Before the sun went down, he woke me up.

'We have reached. This is the town of Thakadur.'

I rubbed my eyes and looked. There were people moving about in the streets. There was no crowding anywhere. People were relaxed, buying the things they needed; it was like a slow-paced song. Some of them were meeting each other on the streets and chatting and then returning home. It must be like this every day here, I thought.

Suddenly, we heard a huge, ear-splitting drum roll. The sound of it sprang on my heart and left me dazed. The horse stopped in its tracks, as though it had received a warning. Makeeran too looked puzzled for a moment. The street, which had looked so placid till then, was now full of people trying to flee, as though the street had caught fire.

'What's this?' I asked in a trembling voice.

'Don't know . . . those are the drums of war . . . we will know soon enough.'

Another war? Was I fated to see conflict wherever I went?

Makeeran could feel my inner terror. He held me as close as he could.

'Such things are common here. Our king is a warrior. But we will not suffer.'

My heart was still stormy. Makeeran said nothing more. He loosened the reins. The sounds of the war drums grew more and more distant.

The horse stopped in front of a hut thatched with grass. The front yard was neglected, covered with dry leaves. A small, run-down cowshed stood next to it. We were at a place which had not been lived in for years. Makeeran pushed open the door. When the sunlight and air fell upon things that had been locked up inside since a long time ago, a rotting smell rose up from them and shrouded us.

From now this was to be my home. The weapons — swords, spears — mounted on the walls had lost their sheen and were covered with cobwebs. Pots and pans, covered with soot, lay scattered and disordered. I began to arrange them in order, but Makeeran stopped me.

'I do not set anything in order,' he said.

'So, to stay here, one must be a thing covered with threadbare cloth?'

He laughed.

'No, not that. I have just got used to this life. No time to tell you more about that now!'

War cries were rising from somewhere in the distance. From far away somewhere, but loud enough to be heard. I was ill-fated. Nothing good took root where I went.

I did not say that aloud. I could not help remembering each thing that had happened after we set out for this place. Were all the tiny wicks of life dying one by one? Was there nothing to do but to carry on till they were all dead?

A spider clambered up and down my leg. I did nothing.

Nine

I went to bed, but could not sleep. Whenever I closed my eyes, the sharp tip of a sword bored through my eyelids. Makeeran was sitting outside, speaking with someone. Some palace attendant, maybe. I felt Makeeran's hand fall on me, gentle and heavy, only after I had dozed off. He embraced me, but his mind was far away. In the battlefield, probably.

'What happened?'

'Always remember that whatever I tell you must stay between us . . . In the time we were away, there was a cattle raid. Our king raided the cattle of another ruler. They are now camped below the hill, seeking to take the animals back. That's what the war drums were about. We will have to go to battle soon.'

I could not say a word. Makeeran wiped the tears that flowed down my cheeks with his lips.

'Don't weep. I have never been defeated in battle. It is you who must hold me up from now.'

'You have to leave in the coming days?'

'Any time now. Tomorrow our king is throwing a war feast for the soldiers. I must go. You must come with me.'

'Me? What for?'

'That's how it is. The warriors' women come too. I am not an ordinary soldier. I am one of the generals. You must be by my side.'

The layers of my new life were beginning to unfold. Many new responsibilities. But this! To hail the warrior setting out for slaughter! To be the source of strength for him to slay his enemies! I thought of their women too . . . and what is a woman who knew little else other than dance and music to do in war? The sight of blood made me feel dizzy. I used to faint at the sight of the severed head of a butchered bull. I hated war, all of it. How was I to go along? I had not thought of this at all when I chose to be with a soldier.

'All this must be new to you,' said Makeeran. 'Don't worry, you will get used to it. In the middle of a battle, I am all alone. If your heart is with me, that is the greatest assurance.'

'I will come with you.'

Ah, do I not continue to walk in spaces that are not mine at all?

Our horse trotted on through a path flanked by cherunthi and churappunna trees. The air was fragrant with the scent of the fallen cherunthi blossoms. The path led to the palace. It ought to have reeked of blood, I thought.

The cowherds and the helots who crowded on either side of the path hailed their king: 'Glory to Athiyaman Neduman Anchi, the king of Velir!'

Makeeran's voice joined them. My throat refused to let out any sound.

We reached the great yard in front of the palace. Alert guards patrolled it. Soldiers were arriving from all over. Though many were coming in, the yard, almost as big as a great common ground, still looked roomy enough for more. We entered a building as big as a hill. There were guards inside too, but their numbers were fewer. The warriors' women were there. The men hailed the king's name loudly. The women ululated.

Soon, the sound of war drums was heard outside. Many kinds of paras and kuzhals accompanied it. The men fell silent; they were straining their ears to know when the royal entourage would enter the building. The king soon appeared under his white, regal umbrella, flanked by women bearing fans of peacock feathers. When the lamplight fell on the pearls of his crown, it seemed as though the Lord of the Day himself had risen in the palace. He wore the royal pana necklace. A golden warrior's anklet shone on his leg, and he carried a long lance. After a moment of awestruck silence, the warriors began to shout his praises again.

'All hail Athiyaman Neduman Anchi, lord of Kuthiramala! May his reign be eternal!'

The king went through the door opposite the grand entrance through which he had marched in. His generals followed him. Makeeran went with them. After some time, they called out the names of some of us waiting in the hall. I went in, reluctantly, when my name was called, along with others. We were summoned to a large pavilion. Its floor was covered with fine white sand. On one side, numerous weapons of war – arrows, bows, swords, shields – were stacked.

Only a few people stood around inside. Serving pots of cooked rice and mutton were placed on a high shelf. Fermented brew bubbled in large mud pots. The king went towards them. A palace attendant drew a cupful of the brew and gave it to him.

When he was about to taste it, a strident voice rose: 'Mazhavar Perumakane! Oh great son of Mazhavar, wait!'

The king drew back abruptly. The voice belonged to an old woman. A wizened female form, its hair all grey, with a face that shone with goodness. Who is this woman who has the power to stop a king? From where did she find the courage to fling her trembling words at the king and stop him?

I did not have to think for long.

'My lord, you must drink only after this general.'

She was pointing to Makeeran!

'It was his ancestor who willingly embraced death, throwing himself before the arrows aimed at your revered grandfather, in a battle long ago. If you are kind, he too will serve you like a sturdy umbrella in the pouring rain. You must eat or drink only after he tastes your food.'

The king smiled.

'Don't you always sift the good from the bad? Are you not beside me to guide me always towards the good, Avva?' he said. 'I will offer no words in reply. Only acts that obey.'

Avvaiyar! Tears gathered in my eyes. Her lines flashed through my mind.

Village or the wild,
A hole or a pile,
If good folk reside in you,
Blessed indeed are you!
Live long, my land!

Before me was the fabled Avvaiyar who had sung so many songs of virtue and goodness! Was there a king who did not yearn for her songs of praise? It was she who had praised Makeeran thus. I felt that my repute in the world had suddenly risen and touched the sky.

Makeeran saluted the king, took the cup that he held out, and sipped the brew. The other generals hailed him.

'There are other brave warriors here. Fill their cups too,' Avvaiyar suggested.

The king beamed. The soldiers began to push their way into the pavilion. Soon, the pots of brew were empty. Giddy bravehearts began to sing drunken praises of their king and dance. They held on to their cups even as they feasted on the meat, rice and curries. The cups were filled as they were emptied and emptied as they were filled.

Avvaiyar busied herself, talking and laughing with the men. She sang praises of each and every one of them.

The soldiers danced with her. I was perplexed. What was there to be so glad about? Maybe it was awe about war, or warm feelings for the men who set out for battle without a thought for their lives.

'Do you not hear the battle cries of our foe? Beat our drums of war!' someone shouted.

With that, the soldiers' excitement reached a feverish pitch. The generals struggled to control them. Makeeran was standing not far away. When he bellowed 'Forward!' I quaked. In a blink of an eye, the pavilion was deserted. The arms stacked there also vanished. They now hid in quivers and armour, tongues sticking out in the thirst for the blood of unknown people.

Now there were just a few women in the pavilion. They must be weary of seeing many battles by now. Some young women were struggling not to weep. Why was I not weeping? One of my two inner selves was probing the other. Maybe the other one was cowering under that needle-sharp gaze which dug out even the innermost feelings. One of them might finish off the other. Perhaps that would be the day I opened myself up to laughter or tears freely. Or maybe reach an inner state beyond wounds or caresses. It would be then that I began to live without expecting either harmony or discord from life. Which of my selves was it that both craved for such a time and feared it?

It was dark soon. Returning to the hut was not possible. The other women seemed to be in no hurry to leave, either. I did not know what to do. Avvaiyar suddenly appeared by my side.

'You are Makeeran's woman? What is your name?'

'Yes, Chithira,' I mumbled, overcome by confusion at her sudden appearance.

'He's told me about everything, after he met you. I just forgot your name.'

I wanted to retort: in songs, the only ones worth naming are the kings! But I just smiled.

'Don't go back to the hut now. It will be difficult. Let's stay here with the other women.'

I nodded in agreement. She moved on to another person. I would have loved to speak more with her. But that could wait.

It was very late, but the women were not sleeping. They sat together in small circles and shared stories about their husbands' valour in combat. They must have heard the war bards sing. How can the battlefield be the object of pride for the warriors' women? Maybe this was how they had learned to cope with their pain.

I did not feel like joining them. I unrolled a mat and lay down. Sleep evaded me. A battle was rolling inside me. Someone was leading. Someone barred the way. The cattle mooed. Someone screamed.

Ten

Makeeran and his comrades returned victorious from the battle after a couple of days. A cow was sacrificed for the female deity that abided in the neem tree and its blood was sprinkled on the tree. The flesh was cooked and shared in a feast.

This time, the king rewarded Makeeran with ornaments of gold. I found out that very evening that he had hidden them away from me in a cloth bundle under his weapons. I was not trying to look for them; I found them when I was trying to clean up and arrange all that he had brought back. I left the bundle where it was with a faint smile and pretended not to know. Maybe he wanted to give me a surprise? I thought he would put them on me when we were together. But four or five days passed, and it did not happen. He continued to behave like a rough soldier at home too; that irked me. But I did not utter a word about it.

I had also begun to take pride in his achievements. Avvaiyar had praised him at the palace. It was the king who had poured him the very first drink of the feast. One day, remembering all this, I asked: 'You never told me about how your ancestor had protected the king's grandfather?'

Makeeran was oiling his weapons.

'That's not my achievement. I don't wallow in whatever my ancestors may have gained. I need to be proud only of what I have achieved on my own.'

'Avvaiyar praised you because of your ancestors, you didn't object then?'

I said that light-heartedly, but Makeeran flew into a rage. He had been oiling a spear. He plunged its sharp tip into the ground and went off in a huff. His leg hit the bowl of ghee which had been used to clean the spear. The liquid splattered on the ground. I was taken aback, nearly struck dumb.

Though he came back after the rage had abated, his face was still dark. From then on, I was careful about what I spoke. I knew that such caution opened up a gap between us. But after that I did not have the strength to ask him anything about him openly.

Makeeran was rarely at home. He would be away for days, frequently, staying somewhere else. This was how it was from our earliest days together. He would not tell me where he was going or why. I would not ask, either. He seemed to hide much. If I tried to find out more it made him furious. I had faith in his love for me. But I did feel the unease of living with someone who could change into an enigma any time.

When he was away, I would often walk outside. Our neighbours were mostly soldiers. Makeeran had told me not to get close to any of their women, so I would exchange a few pleasantries with them and go towards the town. Walking through the town at a leisurely pace, with no everyday cares to bother me, losing myself in each sight, made time fly. The town had many rich people. But that did not reflect in their behaviour.

There was nothing that one could not buy in the market there. From paint and flowers and rouge to precious coral and gold that the merchants brought from faraway places, everything was available. I found long pieces of cane that looked like flutes in a shop. If you removed their thick skin, they were pure sweetness.

'This is sugarcane. One of the ancestors of our king brought it to earth from the heavens!'

One of the shopkeepers was bragging in Athiyaman's name. It must have come from some land far away. I had never seen it before, anyway. Walking through the streets that were not the busy market streets brought me inner clarity. I left the market streets and turned into the vellaalar street. Turning a corner, I heard someone singing – an aged but ringing voice. I recognized instantly the old woman who was sitting by the wayside. Avvaiyar! Some passers-by were offering her coins. The songs which had enchanted even the king – were they to spill so carelessly on the wayside? Stunned, I went up to her quickly and bowed. When I felt her hands press softly on my head, I sank down to the ground and sat down.

'You are Makeeran's woman Chithira, aren't you?' she asked.

Avva remembered me! I felt a sudden thrill. My reply got stuck in my throat.

'What are you doing here?'

'Nothing. I was just taking a walk.'

'Come with me if you have the time.'

Avva got up and began to walk. I followed her. After some time we reached a stone pavilion. She sat down next to a pillar and pointed to the seat next to her.

'What are you doing here, Avva?'

The amazement that I had tucked away revealed itself.

'I am here most of the time. Poets should never be lured by the easy life in palaces. They should see places of hardship and be there, too.'

'Maybe those who have seen nothing but hardship will think otherwise?'

The retort did not anger her. She turned to me with kindly eyes.

'The real reason behind sorrow is wealth. I have wandered in many lands. While in the land of the uzhavar, I drink their rice gruel. In the land of the idayar, I drink their milk and eat plantains! I am a wandering seeker; I do not amass anything.'

Avvaiyar paused.

'My daughter, all I know about you is that you are Makeeran's woman. You are also Mayilan's sister, aren't you?'

I started violently.

'Did Makeeran tell you about Annan too?'

'I know Mayilan. I have met him.'

I was overcome with astonishment. Something strangled me, like a rope – either the shock of hearing the unexpected, or the eagerness to know more about my brother.

'Where? How did you meet him?'

'I go to many places on behalf of the king. Makeeran accompanies me as a guard. I met Mayilan when he was with Makeeran.'

'With Makeeran?'

I felt the world was spinning around me. So Makeeran knew Annan? He had never told me about it!

'Yes, with Makeeran. Mayilan is his friend, isn't he? Yes . . . I remember. That's what he told me then.'

'Please tell me,' I implored her. 'When did you see Annan?'

'My dear, why, you are upset! Did not Makeeran tell you anything?'

I could not find any words. Avvaiyar stroked my back.

'I don't know if I should tell you what Makeeran hasn't . . .'

'Avva, I do not want to know anything . . . I don't even ask where Makeeran goes . . .'

'I don't know why he hid this from you. I'll tell you what I know. I once had to go to the Chera lands as our king's go-between. You probably know, our king is a vassal of the Chera king. I had to go only up to the boundaries of the Chera lands. There the Mighty Three were meeting. Cheraman Maavanko, Pandya Ukkirapperuvazhuthi and Chozha Perunarkkilli, all in the same place! My mind brightened – who would not feel relieved to see three rivals for power come together? Hope gathered in my mind that the terrible wars that shake Tamizhakam might come to an end. Ah, that's another matter! Let me come to the point – that is where I met Mayilan, who was with Makeeran. He came up to me when he saw me. We did not speak much, but I remember him clearly. He looked a bit loutish, but seemed to have a good heart. I don't forget such people. Then Makeeran told me about you, after one of his meetings with you, that you are Mayilan's sister.'

'Avva, we left our homeland to search for Annan. Makeeran knows very well that we have walked endlessly, for very long distances, seeking him. But he did not tell me that they were comrades! I am not able to speak with him – my sadness overwhelms me. There is much that I don't know . . .'

A great flood within swept off most of my heart. Whatever that remained seethed and bubbled in pain.

'Avva, where is Annan now?'

My voice faltered. Tears flooded my eyes at the memory of Achan who gave up his life for Annan, and the thought of Amma whose hair had been chopped off. The anger I felt towards Annan and Makeeran threatened to scorch my eyelashes.

'I know nothing of him since that meeting, my daughter,' Avva said.

'Avva, can I come and see you again sometime?'

Avvaiyar held me close.

'Yes, you must! Come whenever you have the time. Now go. Go back home and rest.'

I did not want to leave. There was so much to find out. I had no home. Makeeran's house was not my home. It was just a rest house which strangers shared occasionally.

I still went back. The house filled me with misgivings. When I unbolted the door and entered, the weapons resting in the corners of the rooms and on the walls grimaced at me. Though they had been polished many times, the awful odour of blood still hung in the air. I felt my head spinning when the piercing stench forced its way into my nostrils. I sank down on the floor. I wanted to wail, but my voice would not rise. I must have spent a long time there, leaning on the wall, eyes shut.

If Makeeran and Annan were friends, then all that had happened till now was a planned charade, set up for someone's benefit. I tried to recall everything that Makeeran had told me since we met. Lies, all of it! Nothing had happened by accident. Even his love for me was pretence, for some other end! All that had happened from the incident at Vel Paari's abode to my travelling here with Makeeran — an unseen someone held the strings of it all. I was a pawn in that game. I was not sure which pawns would survive when the game ended. I might be cut down, like Achan. Or my life might drain away, like Amma's.

Night fell. I had not cooked any food. Nor did I want to eat. I could not lie down. The shadow play of ghouls took over the wall. Like a soldier captured by the enemy, I glanced fearfully at everything around me. The weapons mounted on the wall glinted menacingly when the moonlight fell on them. When I closed my eyes, the shadows brandished spears and seized me by the neck.

This night. Or me. If only one of these would end!

Eleven

I wanted to run to Avva the very next day. It was the thought of a refuge to which I could run any time that was holding my spirit to my body. I managed to kill time till noon and set out only when the light was beginning to recede. Avva was at home. A broad smile, unsullied by her wrinkles, welcomed me to her home.

'What brings you?'
'Nothing.'

'That's good! Are you better?'

I was silent. I only stared at the bamboo pillars that stood between the walls.

'Pain comes along with living with a man. Not to say, living with a soldier. My good luck was that I saw this early. I glance at men only from a distance, always!

'I know nothing of you, Avva. I have listened to your songs. I can sing some of them. Each time I have sung them I have felt warmth for myself rise up within me.'

'My daughter, there isn't much to know. Like anyone else, I too ended up here at the end of a struggle with life . . . Neduman Anchi gave me refuge. He has showered on me kindnesses, more than towards anyone else. Do you know? The day I came here, there were many poets and seekers of benevolence waiting to see the king. Everyone sang his praises. He gave them all many presents. I too sang some songs of praise about him. They seemed to please him, but he bestowed neither a good word nor any presents. I was certain that my words shone with both wisdom and craft. Perhaps because of that, I felt insulted that day.'

The king, responding thus to Avvaiyar's poetry? I could not contain my dismayed astonishment. Now I wanted to hear the whole story.

'My strength is my word, which has a sharp edge. It can polish and sharpen; it can also cut and slice. I would not tolerate disrespect towards it. My body shook with rage. As I stormed out, I addressed the guard at the door aloud, "Hear me, oh sentinel! You are one who does not close the door even against beggars who come seeking refuge. So what? Does not Neduman Anchi know who he is? Does he not know who I am? This is not a world bereft of wise and famous heroes. Do you not know that those who go to the woods with an axe will know no want? If they can't chop down one tree, then another will yield. If not here, then somewhere else. We will eat our rice somewhere."

'As I walked towards the door, someone called out to me. I turned and saw the king's genial smile. You must find this strange, daughter – he had wished to dismiss all others with presents, but he wanted me to stay in the palace. That was why he had given me no gifts. That was his intention.'

Avva's unblemished smile made me smile too.

'The king is a brave man. And endowed with a kind heart too. Athiyaman Neduman Anchi is like a chariot-spoke built in thirty days by a craftsman skilled enough to make eight chariots in a week. A well-built chariot can roll on any road. Once, when the king went hunting, he found a very special kind of gooseberry. A rare and potent life-enhancing treasure. He gave it to me alone. Children's prattle may be nonsense, but it delights us because of our love for them. Anchi's partiality to my songs must be something like that.'

Oh, Avva! Just a little while back she was taking pride in her razor-sharp words. And now, when she was talking of the king's rewards, she was reducing her poetry to childish prattle!

I smiled wryly. Avva sensed its meaning.

'It's like that, my child. When someone puts down our work, our pride is roused. But when we are recognized, we feel that we have not done anything special at all! Anyway, I have not known greater goodness than from Anchi. When I settled here, the responsibilities piled up. I think he does not want me to leave at all.'

'My life too was upturned from trying to find a patron . . . meet a king.'

Avva was keen to hear me. So I told her the whole story. Whenever my voice broke, she caressed me tenderly. By the time I finished, I was lying in her lap. I learned what it was to be called makale – daughter – from her fond touch.

As I lay there, I felt like asking a mischievous question.

'Avva, the king is madly in love with you, isn't he?'

She broke into a merry laugh.

'Not like that. A friend beyond compare. Kin beyond kinship. He to me and I to him.'

Then she paused for a moment, and said, 'But I have once felt as you insinuate . . .' She winked smilingly, and actually looked younger than me.

'That was when he came to see his firstborn, Ezhini. In his battle armour, holding high the spear, a warrior anklet on his leg. Sweat pouring down his body, his neck scratched from battle and stained with blood. The vedchi and venga flowers of victory in his thick, flowing dark curls. Like an elephant risen from combat with a tiger – truly magnificent! He was filled with fond tenderness for his newborn son, but anger towards the enemy still flashed in his eye! Oh, the way he strode in! Seeing him thus I did feel what you hinted!'

It was I who broke into a laugh this time.

It was late when I reached home. Being all alone brought back troubling memories. My inner eye was tormented; the house became a tent of nightmares. I must escape these shadows that creep and sway on the wall. I wanted out. Light. Clear sound. For me, Avva was all of this now. I ached for morning to come so that I could rush to her side. What a woman she was! The more I knew about her, the more I was in awe of her. I remembered her story about how she went as an emissary of Athiyaman to the powerful Thondaman, known for his well-stocked armoury and massive army. She had such a naughty expression when she told me of it! Thondaman received her and gave her a tour of his fabled armoury. Pretending to be wonderstruck, she made up a song about the weapons wielded by Thondaman and Athiyaman and sang it.

These?
Decorated with peacock feathers and garlands,
Bright bodies polished with clarified butter,
Kept safe in the rooms of the palace.
And those?
Because they rain upon the bodies of foes
Their bases are fallen, tips are broken
And they lie forlorn in some tiny ironsmith's hut
Waiting to be repaired.

'It could pass off for a song of praise. Did Thondaman sense its veiled meaning?'

When I asked her, she chuckled, as usual.

'Will Thondaman dare to provoke a battle after this? Athiyaman covered me with gifts when he heard the song.'

I smiled in memory of her delight. I had a sudden urge to sing that song. There were only weapons around me, no lute or drum, so I began to sing, keeping the beat with my hand. But something moved outside. A bolt of lightning passed through me when I stepped out for a quick look.

It was Chanthan.

For a little while, I could not find words.

'I did not think we would meet again. But I had to come. Don't draw back on seeing me! Here, Ulakan has come too.'

Ulakan was lingering on the path outside. I did not ask him to come inside. After a few moments, he too came into the front yard.

'You must come with us.'

It was Chanthan who said that.

I was really surprised.

'Why, what happened?'

'I don't know what to say . . . I will tell you on our way back.'

'No, tell me first. I'll decide whether to come with you or not after.'

'Chithire, nothing happened as we had hoped. It seems that no one will be kind to us, ever.'

'Tell me, what is it? All of a sudden?'

My anxious queries tumbled out as broken words.

I did not ask them to sit, but they both sat down on the veranda.

'Give us some water.'

I came back with water and Chanthan began to speak.

'We went to Muchiri in the land of the Chera. Our journeys by foot are all the same. We reached there, exhausted, but could not meet the king. We were at a loss. A paanan who had settled down there helped us. He found us a place to stay for some days. We spent a few days there. Then, completely unexpectedly, we ran into Mayilan.'

Chanthan paused and glanced at me. Then he continued, a little reluctantly.

'We tried to meet the king. The palace attendants would not let us in. Maybe because we are Mayilan's folk. He must have told them not to let us in.'

I did not utter a word. Did not even show my bewilderment.

'Mayilan saw me, but he tried to slip away. I stopped him and told him of all that had happened till then. I begged him to help us meet the king. But he would not say anything. And he slunk away from me when he got a chance. It is impossible to know his mind . . .'

Chanthan stopped. Then he asked me, 'Why do you not speak? Do you also know about it?'

'No, I am only getting to know . . . whatever I heard is not good . . .'

'What I am going to say is not good either. Makeeran and Mayilan know each other.'

'That I got to know just now. After Makeeran left.'

He did not ask how. He was in a hurry to finish what he was saying.

Ulakan must have been irritated, because nothing seemed to ruffle me.

'We shouldn't have come here . . .' he murmured loud enough for me to hear.

'I don't know about their minds. All I know is that I have been caught in a trap – that I have been betrayed. I know nothing. Makeeran has told me nothing. What did you do after?'

'Everyone wanted to return. We stopped them. We will not return, we said, without finding out what had happened and what was happening. We have no idea what we can do in Muchiri, but our people are staying there. They are waiting for us to fetch you.'

'I am not coming with you. Let Makeeran come when he wants to. I will continue to stay here.'

Chanthan and Ulakan looked at each other. Then, preparing for the worst, Chanthan said, 'All right, do you also know what I am going to say? Makeeran has a woman there; he stays with her. What is the use even if he returns?'

That felled me. I could not reply. I leaned on the wall and tried to hold on to a bamboo pillar for support. My fingers slipped on it. I sat down on the floor. Not that I had expected much from Makeeran. Yet this was hard to bear. I can't recall now why it felt so bad then, though. Because I saw Makeeran in this new light? Because it seemed that he did not see any inner beauty in me, that he craved only my outer charm? Or because I heard this from Chanthan? But this was the moment when I had to be strong.

'I am a woman who left everything behind for an uncertain life. I am not going to return. Did we not meet uzhavar who came home after spending the night with pleasure women? I'll find peace thinking of him as such a man.'

'We know that you are loath to come with us. But what about your life here?'

'I have nothing to consider . . . Did you people have the same concern about my life when I came away? Were you not in a hurry to leave, not bothered about leaving me all alone there? I know the meaning of this visit too. It is a kind of gloating, a kind of revenge.'

'Revenge? What are you saying?!'

'Gloating at my plight . . . at the plight of a woman whose resolve you disliked. No, I was not wrong. This pretence of affection won't work with me.'

Chanthan held back Ulakan, who lunged at me.

'We won't linger here. We are going back.'

They marched out. I did not feel like calling out to them, please come back. Hurrying back into the house, I searched for the gold jewellery under the pile of weapons. Just as I thought – they were not to be found.

Closing the door lightly behind me, I stepped out. There was nothing in that house that I could carry with me as my own. It belonged entirely to someone else. The shadows and nightmares that crept up and down its walls were not mine. Now I felt the radiance within. I felt the lightness of the empty hand. I knew where to go.

I reached Avva's home. Noting that something was wrong, she stood up. That was unusual. I went up to her, knelt down and clasped her knees close to my chest. Avva tried to move away.

'Can I please join you, Avva? Can I walk with you singing your songs?'

'What happened, my girl?'

I told her everything.

'Chithire, the real cause of your pain is not Makeeran's seeking another woman. I know that one can scarcely be with a man who can't be trusted. I can now recall each and every one of Makeeran's moves. Nothing happened by chance. From what I learned and what you said, one thing is certain: you and your people were pawns in a deadly game that he and Mayilan planned together. Even if unwittingly, I too have been part of it, that is over. I will never tell you to go back to Makeeran. If you can't return to your kin, then I won't ask you to. You are welcome to stay here.'

My eyes, which had welled up over and over, were dry now. I hugged Avva.

'Makeeran will indeed return. His future is now certain. I also feel this: the Chami you encountered at Parambumala was most probably your brother. Anyway, you should just forget it all. You may come inside now.'

'My eyes can see now, Avva. I am a woman who could not make a home even though I had a husband. I want to know nothing about Makeeran or my brother. I am not going anywhere. I can't leave!'

III
Mayilan

One

I am not Chami, I am Mayilan. The treacherous son who turned a blind eye towards his wounded father in the throes of death. He who slipped away from his own kin when they were sinking into a mire of distress. The wayward boy who flung aside the tender green shoots cooked without salt by his hapless mother so that he would not starve. Yes, they are all me, Mayilan.

In my childhood I knew nothing but wretchedness. My body was always burning inside and out, like sandy wastes in the height of summer. When the heat of that inner summer scorched my eyes and that sunscald left me blinded, I ran away from home.

The forest was burning that day. The fire spread on the dry leaves piled under the still-green trees; its tongues leapt up till they reached above the crowns of the trees. The relentless wind swished around, feeding the fire, spreading it, taking it even higher. The trees still stood, consumed bit by bit by the conflagration, charred to their very roots. Bison and leopard fought for a way out of the raging fire, dragging away their half-burned bodies desperately. The fire-forged slippers for their hooves and feet; they collapsed in flight. Birds dropped from the sky, their wings ablaze. They fell to the ground and thrashed about in agony.

When the green forests that had swaddled us were finally reduced to a blackened wasteland, I sat down on a rock amidst the billowing fumes and wept inconsolably. There was no desire to bid goodbye to anyone. I will go as far as I can, I resolved. Hardening my heart, I walked away.

The pitiless summer had wiped away all shade from under the trees. The trees thrust out their ravaged limbs, like the broken bones of skeletons. The dust on the reddish path rose up in clouds even before one's foot fell on it. I kept running. Far, far, farther away . . . I thought of nothing else. I walked up the hills and came down into the valley. My breath grew heavier. My legs grew stiffer. The darkness seemed to rush into my eyes. My head swam. Somewhere on the path, I collapsed senseless.

Some wayfarer revived me with water. I did not bother to explain anything to anyone, only dragged myself on. When a familiar face appeared, I would hide in the thickets or in a clump of trees. I crossed the river by sitting on the wooden bridge and shuffling towards the other bank. I was soon away from known lands and faces.

Being in alien lands revived me. I grew strong enough to beg for food when hungry. And I walked on.

This could not last. I had to stop when I reached a seemingly boundless sandy terrain. It was daunting, but I could not return.

Dance and music, which had given us nothing but indigence, repelled me. I must amass coin! Become rich! But this would not be easy, I knew even then. So I did not lose heart. I continued to walk.

The blinding sun and the searing heat were more than I could bear. Strong gusts of wind swept the dust into my eyes, blinding them. My thighs bled from being pricked by thorn bushes. Jagged stones on the ground made my feet bleed. I could not walk any more; there was no shade under which I could rest. When I finally sank down to the ground, I saw death ahead of me.

But I did not die. A group of maravar restored me to life.

'Who are you?' One of them asked. 'Where are you going?'

I told them all.

'Don't go anywhere now. You can live here.'

And so I became one of the maravar, a member of a band of bandits. That is, I joined the people who crouched behind rocks with bows and arrows. We maravar hid ourselves and waited by the wayside – both by day, when the searing sun and pressed on our bodies like a massage-bundle of smouldering coals, and at night, when the biting cold knit itself into the very folds of our skin.

Our leader was called Chothi. Firm-bodied, with a head full of dark curls and a leopard's stare, he cut an imposing figure. When he came into our midst, silence reigned. No one dared to even whisper anything against him. I feared him much, but also adored his strength.

'Treat all the people who end up here alike.' That was Chothi's view. 'If you try to get to know your victims, you'd want to spare them all. You'll feel sorry for all alike. Also we would start bickering among ourselves about how to treat them. Never quarrel among ourselves for the sake of others. Kindness and tenderness should be among us, not towards others. Never forget that we have vowed to stay together for life.'

The leader's word was the word of command. We seized everything we found on our victims, irrespective of whether they were well-endowed men of wealth or beggars who lived from day to day. Raid just enough to save ourselves from the terrible chill of the night, Chothi used to say. We spared the fear-stricken folk who flung before us all their belongings; they would be scared away. We didn't think twice about killing those who resisted us.

One night, we were replanting the desert scrub. The plan was to plant it on both sides so that the space between would look like a path running through the wayside thickets of a village. It was a ruse to make travellers lose their way and end up right in front of us.

We set up pandil lamps on either side of the 'path'. They were filled with oil and readied with cotton wicks, then placed in mud basins fixed on bamboo stands. Soon, we saw a figure coming up the 'path'. On one shoulder was a curved kavadi pole on which hung some mud pots and vessels. A stick, as long as a man's body, rested on his other shoulder. The garland he wore around his neck seemed twined on the stick.

'That's an ascetic! A world renouncer! He probably owns nothing,' one of my comrades whispered to me.

'Get away from here!' another of us roared at him.

The man seemed least bothered. He began to pull up some of the bushes that we had planted.

'What is he doing?!'

Chothi rushed towards him.

'It is fair for the starving to take from the rich. But deception is not a virtue!'

He continued to do what he was doing.

Suddenly, something, like a massive breaker, crashed inside me. My nerves grew taut. On a sudden impulse, I dashed towards him, pounced on the stick he held and began to thrash him with it.

'Mayila! No!'

Even Chothi was astounded by this version of me.

I stopped. The others helped him up. As he walked away bloodied, he glowered at me. His look cut to the quick.

I ran back to our camp in the distance and fell, frustrated, face down, on a mat.

After a little while, something moved. It was Chothi.

'Never mind . . . I know you did that because you were told to treat all our victims in the same way. But as far as possible, do not harm ascetics.'

In many later incidents too, I showed myself to be immature. Though I feared that Chothi would punish me for my impulsiveness, nothing of that sort happened. On the contrary, on such occasions he treated me with greater kindness. It was he who taught me how to shoot an arrow and instructed me in the basics of swordsmanship. I practised my aim with cattle which strayed into our area, and swordplay with my comrades. And became somewhat skilled in both. Even when I felt that my fingers, which had once played the lute and the drums, would not lend themselves to wielding weapons, I persisted. I was not willing to let go of what I had learned newly.

In a gang it was easy to become brash. My hands were no longer shy of violence and murder. I acted in utterly pitiless ways, but my esteem for our leader made me all the more enthusiastic. Life among the maravar more or less erased my past. If the notes of a song flitted into my mind by chance when I was sharpening my weapons on some hero stone, I would grab it by the neck and choke it to death before it left my throat.

This life was not to last long. One day, three of us were on our way back from collecting water from a pond far away. We heard the screech of the wheels of a horse cart. As usual, we rushed towards it and threw our spears, which we always carried, at the leg of the horse. They did not hit the target, but the cart stopped. A man leapt out of it. It was evident at the very first glance that this was no ordinary traveller. The lotus garland on his chest swung as his firm, dark body lunged forward. As usual, my comrades ran towards him and pressed the tips of their weapons on either side of his neck. He flicked off the weapons in a flash; two soldiers jumped out of the cart now. This caught my comrades completely off guard; all they could do was flee. I was petrified for a moment, but I too took to my heels. But the soldiers caught up with me and knocked me down; I was simply not fast enough. One of them raised his lance, but the other stopped him.

'Don't. He is very young.'

When I tried to scramble up, a soldier kicked me in the chest. I could not move.

'Tie him up and throw him into the cart!'

One of them brought a rope; they began to tie up my limbs. I tried to wriggle and resist and loosen the rope with my teeth. But nothing worked. They tossed me inside the cart and tied me to a bamboo pillar. The cart sped away, raising clouds of dust.

'Let me go! Where are you taking me?'

They ignored me. I tried to move my limbs, but it was impossible.

After some time, I told them, 'Free me, please. I will do as you say.'

Not being able to move at all was unbearable. But I did not have a destination anyway when I set off. What did it matter where they took me now?

'Untie him,' said the man who sat in the front seat, looking out.

The soldiers untied me.

'Who are you? Where are we going?'

They took their time to answer, glancing at the man. Seeing that he did not object, one of the soldiers told me, 'We are the soldiers of the king of Ezhimala, Nannan. The person who sits in front is Paranar, the great poet.'

Paranar. Some of the songs that Amma used to sing came back to me, but not their verses.

'I have heard of him.'

The soldiers looked surprised. They probably did not expect a marava boy to say that.

'Who are you? What is your name? We will help you if you tell us the truth. But if you lie, your life will be hell.'

'Don't try to scare me,' I retorted. 'I have nothing to lose. I have seen many kinds of hell. I am not afraid.'

Paranar laughed aloud and turned.

'Don't say such things to him,' he told them. 'He must have ended up among the maravar somehow.'

I watched the sights outside as we passed them. When we left the hot wasteland behind, my body and mind both began to cool down. But the abundant green and the moist air did not excite me much. Maybe I had gotten used to the wasteland! I had nothing to do; so I just leaned back, dozing off and waking again as we went past many sights. We went up and down hills and crossed jungles. The warm greetings Paranar received from people when we took breaks to rest the horse and refresh ourselves left me speechless with wonder.

We soon reached the riverbank; rafts built from large logs waited for us there. It was not difficult to get the horse cart on the raft and off it. The boatmen did it expertly. We stopped at homes for meals. I greedily ate up all the delicacies they served. We stayed at an inn for a night. There too Paranar was greeted with much adoration; I felt a stab of envy. The soldiers must have guessed what was on my mind.

'The great poet is as renowned as the king himself. Our king Ezhimala Nannan's bosom friend. Respected by kings wherever he goes. But no matter where he may go, he is sure to return to Ezhimala!'

I was, however, mulling over something else. If I went along with these people, gaining influence with the king might not be a distant dream any more. My mind – it had always dwelled in a palace. Even when I had nothing to do but stare up at the sky in the middle of the barren wilderness. That wish was going to be fulfilled painlessly. My dream had taken a concrete form and was waiting right in front of me.

I felt really amused when I noticed that the guards were indeed guarding me very carefully. I wouldn't run away, would I, even if they wanted me to?

Two

We set off from the inn early at dawn. The wind was chilly. The path was even. The horse forgot its fatigue and dashed ahead. Though the sun began to grow strong, we were still in the encircling arms of the cool breeze. The trees were no longer ones I knew. White sands lay beyond them. In the distance, waves rolled towards the beach.

'The sea!' I shouted, though I had never seen it before. Paranar turned smilingly to me.

The cart got on the tree-lined path towards the beach. When it reached the sand, we got off and began to walk. My feet, which had got used to the harsh sands of the desert, were tickled by the beach sand. The strokes left behind by crabs on the wet sand. The scattered shells of sea creatures. The umanar, the salt makers, were returning home in their bullock carts.

'Where are the canoes of the parathavar, the fisher folk? Where are the umanar's salt pans?' I asked. I felt a comforting fullness within when we found them. I tried to recall the songs I had heard as a child. I had wandered on these shores through them. The salty sea breeze had danced around me once, long ago.

The deep darkness that hung on the sediment heap around the salt pans recognized me.

'Who are you? How did you end up in the marava band?'

It was only then that Paranar asked me something about my life.

It is not pleasant to recall the past – I wanted to put that to him bluntly, but my voice failed me. I opened up and told him everything, from the endless starvation in the huts of the paanar to the cruel deeds of the maravar. By then, I had a fair idea of Paranar's cast of mind. I reckoned that to deal with him, it was better to reveal rather than conceal.

Before Paranar could say anything in reply, I ran towards the shore and clambered up on the rocks on which the waves crashed and shattered. Sitting down, I let my gaze sweep towards the opposite shore, somewhere far beyond our eyeshot. Maybe this world ended there! It must be another world out there, other people! How would life there be? One of want and misery? Or of richness and plenty? My eyes were glued to the horizon; I hardly felt time pass.

Paranar was in a hurry to leave. He stood below, calling me. I glanced lovingly at the waves one more time before I began to climb back down. As we walked, I noticed the white blooms on trees with black scales on their trunks. Paranar told me about the many different kinds of punna trees. Some bear golden yellow flowers.

Then there were the njaazhals, the flowers which had abundant stamens. Amidst them were the blooming mundakan shrubs, screwpine bushes and water thorns. Their tips scraped my foot, but I was not bothered.

We climbed into the horse cart again. As the horse trotted onwards, I kept gazing at the sea through the gaps between the trees. I craved the sight of the infinitely lapping waves. When the sea disappeared from eyeshot, I waited for it to reappear.

'I was not mistaken.'

I heard Paranar tell the soldiers smilingly.

The forests and hills resurfaced as we left the coast. The horse cart ran slower now. A forest in which bright red flowers bloomed. Where there were thick clumps of bamboo. Hordes of wild pigs with tiny eyes. The humble huts of the forest dwellers. Nearby was a large field on which the velar held their veriyaattam. I noticed a number of hero stones – memorials for heroes who perished in combat, said Paranar. There were also many small shrines in the lush groves of karimkoovalam trees.

'These are the shrines of the spirits who protect the hill,' said the soldiers, laughing. 'No one dares touch them. If anyone dares to pick a flower from one of these trees, our king will slice his throat. You are going to be in a very good place!'

I held my tongue and kept my eyes fixed on the sights outside. At all the places where the roads parted, signboards firmly tied to trees showed the way to Ezhimala, making travel easy for the first-time visitor. Before long, we reached the place. I saw the massive fortress and the great door from afar. Along with guards, elephants, dark and menacing as rainclouds, kept watch at the gates. Nearing the place, I saw the deep moats. No one stopped us when we entered.

I never expected such a big city on that hilltop! Many guards patrolled the city streets. With my very first glance at the city I knew that this was a place of strong men and beautiful women. The guards saluted us and withdrew as we moved through the streets. I saw the king's palace at close quarters. In the middle of a spacious yard, there was a long path for chariots, and it was decked with flags. Where it ended, among many-pillared pavilions, was a mansion of many storeys. The king probably lived on the middle floor.

From the time we arrived, we could hear the intermingled sounds of drums and horns and singing.

'What is happening? Are they celebrating a vizhaavu?'

'You could say that. It's dance and music here all the time! The paanar and koothar are always around. The king has never flinched from chopping off the heads of his foes in battle, but he is besotted with song and dance. He may look stern, but our king's heart softens at the sight of paanar and koothar. It's a vizhaavu here every day!'

205

I remembered my people. I had tried to tell them many times that we should leave our home and seek a patron among the kings. They would not budge. Fated to wallow in misery! I gnashed my teeth.

I must gain riches. One could not squander away one's life starving!

I was never a good singer or dancer. And I had mostly forgotten whatever I had learned. What way, then, to earn the king's favour?

I racked my brains, though I was also staring vacantly at the girls clad in colourful waist cloths with fragrant flowers in their hair. They wore many kinds of necklaces on their breasts and jingling bangles on their arms. The young fellows hanging around were busy flirting with them.

Paranar got off at a house almost as big as the palace.

'He doesn't seem to be a troublemaker, but keep an eye on him.'

The soldiers nodded in agreement.

Oh poet . . . I have no intention of going anywhere! Do you think that I am a fool to let this golden chance go, I laughed inwardly.

Some days passed. I stayed with the soldiers. I walked around the town. But the days grew slow and boring. Then I was given a job in the palace, probably on the poet's recommendation. I was to join the gardeners and my job was to water the plants in the palace garden. There were three other workers there.

The poet probably thought this would bring me an income enough for a comfortable life.

But for me this was the first step towards gaining the king's favour. I had to climb up from there. I needed to be careful. Unlike my co-workers, I did not go out in the evening to get drunk or to dance with the virali wenches. I did not let anyone get too close, either. I focused on work. Or pretended to.

Paranar would visit sometimes. Passing me, he would give me a friendly pat.

'Hey, you are a paanan, aren't you? But you know no songs?'

'I am not keen on singing.'

'Then you must learn. Everyone has a pair of eyes. That's not enough. Only those who have another pair – of inner eyes – can claim to see.'

'I would like to learn.'

'Good! Come over to my house sometime.'

Thus I began to visit the great poet.

'Be aware of space and time. Know the good from the bad. You must learn about many kinds of people and their duties. If we do not understand what needs to be understood about our world, then knowledge will itself be wasted.'

Paranar began to speak. It became a regular part of my routine to go to his house when my duties at the palace were over. I began to sense the depth and breadth of language through the alphabet, sound and meaning. Paranar would go off to foreign lands in between. During those gaps, I would practise that which I had learned.

I could soon recognize what was virtuous and what was clever, what was Duty and what was Rule, without referring to any of the memory-keeping phrases. I stored away in my mind all that the poet pointed to as illustrations. But I was most eager to learn about the Art of Ruling – Arichiyal – which taught us the intricacies of power and rule, of how to subjugate the land. Paranar, too, noticed that.

'We don't need to know all that the kings are expected to know. Besides, it is not yet time for you to master the Art of Ruling. But I will give you a general idea.'

I nodded. He stroked my hair affectionately.

'My child, I retrieved you from a band of maravar. It seems certain now that I was not wrong to do so.'

The next day, the royal order reached me. I was made a palace attendant.

Thus I rose from a lowly state to a much higher one. My mind brimmed over with joy.

Three

My task as an attendant was to guard one of the inner doorways of the palace. It was around that time that I first got to behold the king. He was indeed endowed with all the marks of a king, as Paranar had described when he taught me Arichiyal. Though the ruler of a smaller domain, he was a leader capable in all ways: in his fearless army, vast lands, immense wealth, lavish entourage, many able friends and impenetrable fortress. I saluted him and stepped back. He glanced at me. His eyes shone with valour. Did I see a glimmer of affection in them? Paranar must have mentioned me to him. That seemed certain. Or was it just my feeling?

I badly wanted to learn more of Arichiyal. It never left my mind. It seemed to me that it was a good way to rise up from the status of palace guard. I rifled through the poet's palm-leaf manuscripts. I did not see much about Arichiyal there. But I continued to visit him after work.

Sometimes I would walk with him on the seashore. The rhythm of war songs was that of the sea. Paranar's songs and the king's fury in war were both endowed with a power which was like that of the forceful surf that dashed and scattered on the seashore. The waves rolling up and crashing down in quick succession; somewhere in the far distance, beyond the horizon, another shore... my thoughts flew to them. I fell into the habit of staring at the sea even when Paranar was not with me. Looking around, one could see the hilltops on which the peacocks danced. It was said that there were many gold mines around here. The busy city was visible from the shore. So also, on one side, the wagons of the umanar carrying salt descending the hills and making their way to distant lands. This is a land on which the sea bestows pearls, and the hills, rubies. I had indeed reached the right place.

One day, an old man came up to me when I was standing guard inside the palace. I had seen him many times with the king. He was also a palace attendant, and so I became quite friendly with him. We began to run into each other quite often. This time, however, he first made sure that no one was listening and then whispered to me: 'There's going to be an incident in the palace soon. I tried telling the king, but he does not take it seriously.'

It sounded like a strange business. I was caught completely unawares. Why was he telling me this? I asked him precisely that.

'The king's life is in your hands. And in those of the other guards. I am telling them too.'

'I am doing my duty here.'

'That's not enough. You must show your quickness by sensing what needs to be done in advance.'

The summary of what he said was that there was going to be an attempt on the king's life in a couple of days, and this was being plotted by a general named Minjhili.

I was in a fix. I had heard a lot about how loyal this general was to the king. What was I to do? Tell the king directly? And this was being affirmed by none other than a senior attendant in the palace! That evening, the old man approached me again.

'You must do as I say. We cannot trust everyone. The king's life is above all else for us. Two other guards will join you today. They are sworn to protect the king's life. The three of you must slay Minjhili and his men.'

I was standing there looking quite startled and shaken when two guards came to me.

'The old man must have told you? We are also the king's guards. The deed is planned for tomorrow. We have heard that Minjhili and his men will come by this entrance today to prepare for tomorrow. We must take their lives before they cross this gate.'

I did not speak, merely nodded. I did not know what to do, but my mind was racing – something had to be done. I felt that I should meet the poet. But he was not at home. Anyway, I took some of the dried pieces of palm leaf that I had found on his veranda, came back, and wrote down on them all that I had heard. Then I waited for the king to appear. He did not come that way on that day, so I decided that I had to find him.

When I did, he was surrounded by guards, and that made me very wary; but I decided to risk it and approached him directly. I placed my palm-leaf pages before him and stood there, hands folded in salutation. I did not wilt under the scorching looks the guards showered on me. Someone picked up the leaves and gave them to the king. And the king ordered me to leave even before he read them.

'You may leave!'

I bowed to him again and withdrew.

I left the palace and was making my way through the darkness when a group of four or five men surrounded me. I drew my sword and stood alert, ready for any blow. I dealt with their thrusts and broke their circle, leaping forward. My thrusts did not cut them down; they still managed to run away.

The next day, when I was standing on guard duty, Paranar came up to me.

'Excellent move, what you did. A large hurdle has been crossed.'

Paranar smiled and left without saying anything more.

I was baffled when four or five days passed and nothing seemed to have happened. No one congratulated me. The old man and the king's guards were still at their regular tasks and they were still close to the king. This perplexed me no end and upset me too.

The people who came to see the king who passed by this entrance were of different sorts. Some would not even look at me. I would bar the way for such people and pretend to check their things. I would open every gift they brought the king. For the most part, such people were not trouble. My anger towards them was against their refusal to acknowledge my existence.

Those who appeared furtive and sneaky were usually harmless – they just did not how to conduct themselves in a palace. I would just tease them. It was the ones who looked completely proper who made my heart beat hard. If you were not really careful with them, you could even lose your job.

Most of those who came from elsewhere were paanar and koothar. Once, I saw someone who I remembered vaguely from my childhood and began to feel very anxious. I moved away from the door, pretending to not be a guard at all. He came closer. I stood there quietly.

'You look very familiar. Like I have seen you somewhere earlier.'

He stopped, as if to recall.

'Aren't you Mayilan?'

Something flared up inside me. I did not bother to reply. This man was one of my people, I was sure.

'If you are here to see the king, get on with it. I am busy,' I said tartly.

He stopped trying to talk to me. I pretended not to notice how he was carefully measuring me up when he left.

'I too have left home and am now a wanderer. I have been to many places. I will continue to wander. My spirit is fated to pass away in such a manner . . .'

I still did not utter anything. He walked away, looking back a few times.

I realized that he had learned that I was a guard at the palace.

'Don't tell anyone that this is what I do,' I shouted to him from behind. He turned, threw me a severe look, and left.

Very soon, I became a member of the king's retinue. All that had happened, it turned out, was a test devised by those who were close to the king. The general Minjhili too turned an affectionate eye towards me. Only later, when I learned more about spying in Arichiyal, did I realize the full import of these happenings.

Spies. The palace crawled with spies. From the gardeners to the foot soldiers of the king's entourage. The spies did not know each other. Each one spied on the other, and they passed on all that they knew to the king. The king was behind even the decision to promote me. I also saw then why the poet had said that I did not need to know all about Arichiyal.

Within a short span of time, I rose again, from being a mere soldier in the king's retinue. I moved into my own house. I recalled and practised there all that Paranar had taught me. I saw that the king was partial to me – many times. I was born a paanan. I grew up as a maravan. And gained knowledge under an illustrious poet. I took pride in thinking that no king would abandon a man with knowledge, courage and loyalty. I don't remember if I was really loyal to the king. Ultimately, the king was loyal to himself. And I, to myself.

I began to accompany the king on many of his travels. The royal entourage and soldiers would follow. Minjhili was there for the most part, and sometimes Paranar. Paranar's affection for me flowed through the king too, and so I became very easy with them. Nannan, who had conquered by the might of his arms all the lands from Ezhimala to Aanamala, had no time away from war. He who had defeated Pazhayan and Pindan a long while ago went back to battle again and again. Even the Mozhipeyar lands were conquered. It was around that time that I realized that his perspiration reeked of the blood spilled in battle. Whenever I stood behind him in the chariot on the battlefield and the wind blew in our faces, I would open my nostrils and take it in fully.

Sometimes he would emerge mounted on an elephant. This king was so fond of slaughtering his enemies, beheading their elephants and shooting down their horses with arrows – how could he be so enamoured of dance and music when he returned to his palace? It confounded me. My eyes were filled with the sights from the scenes of combat. Warriors soaked in blood. Weapons piercing, cutting, slicing. Bodies writhing in agony. Each time, I would ache to leap into the fray, to wound and be wounded. When victory was certain, the king would step down into the battlefield and dance with his warriors.

Once Nannan went to battle against the rulers of Punnaad in his chariot. His flag flying high and proud. As usual, I went with him. He was a sight to be feared, indeed — with his coat of armour glimmering on his broad chest and the many golden chains flashing on it! The whole of Punnaad trembled before the might of this fearless king. The warriors of Punnaad attacked and defended as best they could, but could not hold on.

A huge army mounted on elephants, their legs like massive pillars, pursued Nannan. As was usual in battle, we moved away from the battlefield and attacked the places settled by people. We took away cattle from the cowsheds of the rich. Our soldiers carried away large bundles of rice and millet from their granaries. Seized their gold and coin. On the way back, we set fire to the grain fields. We took all the booty back to Ezhimala.

The people of Punnaad did not stay quiet. They went wailing about their ruin to many kings. Narmudicheral, of the Chera lineage, heard of the attack. This powerful king, one of the Mighty Three, had heard of our king's exploits and was seething with envy. One of his close confidants, Ay Eyinan, went to Punnaad. We came to know that he bragged to the people there that they were not to be afraid as long as he was alive. Our king became more cautious about war after this. Ay Eyinan was indeed a powerful ruler. And supported by the Chera. A confrontation might be too risky, he must have thought.

All of us now felt that our king had become somewhat tame lately. Paranar was still by his side, trying to instil courage in him. The paanar and koothar made up songs of his exploits. His feats would stay undiminished in the future too – they declared!

A pitched battle was imminent, we all felt, and it came true. Ay Eyinan, along with a large troop, came down to Pazhi and challenged our king to combat. We were ready for them! But our king seemed somewhat dispirited. Minjhili, who arrived in battle array, could not contain his disappointment with our king's lethargy.

'No matter who we clash with, I swear to rip off their heads for a sacrifice on the field of slaughter! I will offer their blood to the ghouls!'

Minjhili and his troop charged vigorously at the foe. Eyinan and his comrades met their charge with valour. Pazhi turned into a sacrificial field. The two armies were evenly matched. The confrontation dragged on and on. Minjhili and Eyinan were locked in direct combat. Minjhili's oath was not in vain! He brought down his mace forcefully on top of Ay Eyinan's head. Eyinan fell dead on the battlefield.

It was a blazing hour. Our warriors, covered in blood and sweat, forgot their fatigue and raised slogans of victory. Eyinan's corpse lay on the scene of carnage in the sweltering heat. Sensing that a distant clamour was overpowering the clanging of weapons on the battlefield, Paranar and I looked up. Up in the sky, birds were circling the battlefield, as though one of their own had been killed! Their numbers kept growing! They soon formed an enormous shield in the sky that shaded Eyinan's body from the blinding sun. Even the warriors drew back in sheer astonishment.

'Eyinan was known to be merciful not just to people but even to birds,' Paranar said, anguished by his death. 'They now give him back that care. They are spreading their wings over him, shielding him from the glowering noon sun.'

He went off to the war tent, where the king was resting, to tell him of the day's happenings. I came to know later from Paranar that the king too was deeply sorrowful at Eyinan's death, and that he did not even come to the battlefield to greet the victorious Minjhili. Nannan, known for his stubborn adherence to his word, was mourning the death of an enemy general! The two sides of a king's mind: music, dance, mercifulness and Paranar on one side; war, cruelty and *I* on the other. The very thought perked me up. I was toiling well, I thought, smiling inwardly.

Minjhili, still overflowing with the fury of combat, seemed quite oblivious to everything. He was dancing the vennikkoothu of victory like one possessed, and blood dripped from the flower garland he wore on his neck. My limbs ached to join the macabre celebration. I stepped in.

The war bards' songs that rose along with the war drums clashed with the sounds of the battlefield. Their descriptions of shattered skulls, dismembered bodies, of ghouls rushing madly, crazed by the scent of blood oozing from the human flesh strewn all around – Minjhili seemed lost in them. The other warriors and I joined hands and danced in that scene of frenzy, which looked like the middle part of hell. Elephants and horses were swept away by the tide of blood that flowed that day, like ships on the seas. Eagles and vultures were tearing open the chests of dead warriors, and ravens swooped down on the ground caked with drying blood.

The war bards sang about all that they saw on the battlefield. Their singing grew louder. 'Ye ghouls! Take the teeth of the fallen and make them your rice, prepare the feast of the vanquished! All Hail the Queen of the ghouls who craves the flesh of the corpse!'

They began to prepare for the field sacrifice. I readied myself. I had to be quick enough to wipe away even a tiny drop of tenderness, if it took shape in my heart. I had to be able to do any dreadful task without flinching.

A hearth was built from the skulls of three heads that had rolled on the battlefield. They found the wood of the koovalam tree to light it. In the human blood that boiled in a large basin upon it, human flesh and intestines bubbled up. The basin was stirred with a severed human head mounted on a stick, the skin peeling off it. A ball of rice and blood was ready soon, and the oracle of the ghouls offered it to the deity of war, Kottavai. The anthanar, well-versed in all four streams of their sacred verse, performed the sacrifice. Those who knew the sacred verse probably did not distinguish between mercy and cruelty!

In the midst of all this, something foamed inside my head furiously and threatened to spill over. All around me were the ghouls. They were grinning and grimacing and thrusting forward their enormous bellies. I was dancing with them. In front of me was a shattered world, fallen to pieces. The terrible wails of the widowed women of the fallen warriors filled my ears. A splintered tusk pierced my foot. Headless bodies covered with blood seemed to rise up from the ground and join the dance. I remember one of the soldiers catching me from falling when I stumbled.

Four

Nannan's fame climbed right up to the sky with his victory at Pazhi. The poet sang many songs about it. It was his fondness and kindness towards me, like the love he bore the king, which worked to my advantage. How was it that the great poet, with all his wisdom, did not see my true self? What would be his response if my manipulations, now concealed deep in my heart, came out someday? I wondered about such things.

Anyway, before long, I became one of the king's close confidants. I had read in many places that the learned would take root in the lands that hosted them. I was inching close to that goal now. Fearing that an inner smile of triumph was threatening to grow into a burst of laughter, I pressed it down. I recollected that Paranar had told me that the essence of Arichiyal lay in the king's embrace of those who possessed knowledge. That was what he probably advised the king too.

I was with the two of them throughout. The king listened to Paranar; knowing that, I positioned myself between them. But it was not to last long.

After the triumph at Pazhi, the king seemed disturbed. Was it because he feared the vengeance of the Chera? Or perhaps he thirsted to rise from the status of a vassal to another king?

One of those days, I had a chance to go to Aanamala with the king. We were accompanied by guards and paanar. I hoped to see some sights from my boyhood on the route, which wound around Poozhinaad. I sought the maravar in the paala wilderness. But the king's troop must have taken another route to capture Aanamala – through forbidding paths that included steep climbs and dense forests. The maravar country was probably accessed from the other side of the hill that lay horizontally, barring the way. The path of war is arduous, though it may seem easy afterwards. If the king wishes to keep a land that is not his, then the challenges are daunting.

For Nannan, this was a journey he undertook regularly. He was diligent about guarding each nook and corner of the land. About settling people's complaints and learning about his enemies' moves and acting before they could.

He was keen to go to Aanamala also because he had a garden of rare mango trees there. He was devoted in his attentions to it. If anyone dared to break a single twig from any tree there, his death was assured.

After we reached the place, the king was busy, as usual, in dealing with complaints and requests from the local people. In between, the keepers of the mango grove came to greet him. It was routine for him to go to the mango orchard each time he visited the place, examine the trees and renew his pride in them. The whole retinue, including Paranar and I, followed him this time. One of the keepers stood waiting for the king. He opened his mouth to speak. The king noticed that the other keepers were gesturing to him to stop. When the man refrained from saying what he was about to say, the king commanded him to speak, whatever the matter was. He obeyed.

He accused a little girl who was bathing in the river below of theft! Apparently, she had dared to eat a fruit from the king's mango grove! The mango had ripened and fallen off its stalk into the flowing waters. She had found it. The king ordered her to be brought before him. In a short while, the little one and her family were brought there. It was evident that they were wealthy. But they were terrified and trembling all over. However, their fear only seemed to feed the king's anger.

'It was not done on purpose! Please forgive us!' They wailed and wept. The little girl, not comprehending anything, looked bewildered.

'The guilty must be punished. Rich or poor, there can be no lenience.'

'It's a child who knew nothing! What is rich and poor for her?'

The king did not like them correcting him.

'The law is that anyone who steals anything from this grove must be punished with the pain of death. That cannot be changed.'

The child's parents and relatives broke into a cold sweat. They flung themselves at the king's feet.

'Please punish us in some other way! In any way!'

'Let those who know the law speak.'

The king looked at us. Paranar was aching to say something. The other advisers seemed confused.

'We will present you a doll of gold of the same weight as her!' The child's relatives kept on mumbling offers. 'We will offer nine elephants besides . . .'

'The law is that those who steal the king's property must die. Nothing can replace it!' I jumped in before anyone else. This was my chance to display my learning before the king, and I was not going to miss it.

My response seemed to give Paranar a tremendous shock.

'What are you saying? Is this not a tender child? A child who knows nothing of the world! I would only say: let the family pay some other penalty.'

'Was it not you who taught me kingly law? It is you who also told me that all offenders should be treated alike by the law!'

'This deed was committed without the intention of breaking the law. You cannot say that it is a crime. She is a little girl! And murdering women brings no glory to the king!'

'Whoever may be the culprit, ascertain the nature of the crime, administer justice without fear or favour. The Arichiyal that you taught me says so!'

'He is right,' the king nodded in assent.

'Murder a child, a little girl, for something she did unwittingly? There are considerations that go beyond that which is written on palm-leaf pages!' Paranar kept arguing.

'Not just on palm-leaf pages, but also in the tales of glory that we have heard about kings. Have you not heard of the Chozha prince Ellaalan? The one who killed his own son for a wrong he committed innocently?' I too continued, making sure that the king was paying attention.

'One day, the large bell that Ellaalan had hung in the yard of his palace for people who came to complain was rung by a cow. It was crying about how its calf had died when the king's little son ran it over with his toy chariot. The king ordered that his son be run over with a chariot to ease the cow's sorrow. When no one came forward to do this deed, he took it upon himself. His glory rests on this deed, my lord.'

The king had no more doubts.

'Nannan's fame is that he treats all offenders alike. This child must pay with her life. I order her death!'

Her loved ones began to wail and weep. Paranar sat with his head bowed.

The great poet must have abandoned the king's company that very day. I came to know that he did not bid farewell even to the king. When we got back to Ezhimala, one of the poet's attendants came to me with a bundle of palm-leaf manuscripts. It was the translation of a book some anthanan had written in the language that the anthanar held sacred. Its title was *Ottaadal*, The Art of Spying.

What was this – a gift of knowledge that I had so coveted? Or the hint of a curse, calling me a spy? Whatever it was, all I thought then was that I had got what I had desired so badly.

After the great poet's departure, I felt that I now held the king in the middle of my palm. Certainly, it was Paranar who had gifted me with knowledge.

But it was inconvenient to have someone like him around all the time. He had so many other admirers among rulers!

The king was deeply affected by Paranar's exit. I tried to fill the void by taking his side on everything. I knew well myself that my selfish counsel could not replace Paranar's impartial and fearless advice. But I was able to create the impression that I was more loyal to him than I actually was.

That balance did not endure. What the king had feared came true. Seeking revenge for the death of Eyinan, the Chera king besieged Ezhimala with a formidable army. As usual, Minjhili worked himself up into a frenzied battle rage and rushed towards the enemy. But the king knew perfectly well that he could do little in the face of a direct assault overseen by the Chera king himself. The face of Nannan, heavy with the portent of defeat, is probably not to be found in any of the songs about him. But I saw it with my own eyes. After we had news that Minjhili was killed, the king would not listen to anyone. Because he was so sullen, none of his advisers dared to approach him. A shadow that could not but be an omen of death had fallen on his face.

He set off for the battlefield, deciding to face the enemy despite the odds. I stopped him.

'It is better to withdraw from the battle. We may not be able to hold out against the Chera king!'

He pretended not to hear. I followed him.

'Please listen! It is my duty to stop you now. My devotion to you endures . . .'

'If only Paranar were by my side . . .' That was the reply. A low murmur.

'Please forgive me if I am wrong. It was Paranar who taught me. A powerful and canny king's withdrawal from battle is like the ram pulling back its legs before head-butting its opponent and flooring it . . . there's no shame in it.'

The king pursed his lips. That was the gesture that fully revealed what he thought of me.

'You are too young . . . it is not enough to know from books alone. You must know the land, and other lands too. That is Paranar's great strength. If he were with me, I would have asked him to be my emissary to the Chera king. His words cannot be set aside even by the Mighty Three.'

I had no answer.

'I am leaving to fight with no hope of return,' said the king. 'The king's pride lies not in running away, but in fighting to the finish.'

Nannan left with his warriors. I was stopped when I sought to go with him. But he did not go to the battlefield. I heard whispers later that he had hidden himself somewhere in the impenetrable eastern forests.

I had misjudged the king. He knew the Arichiyal much better than I did!

After that I was not foolish enough to tarry in that land.

Five

When I left Ezhimala, I bundled up everything I had accumulated till then and carried it with me. In the palace, my meals had been taken care of. I had even managed to save a bit. I had hoped to amass some wealth as the king's chief adviser, but the king had absconded before I could manage that!

It was not easy to escape unnoticed from a city surrounded by enemy soldiers. I managed to get a yaazh and a para from a paanan and made my way out of the city. I came downhill disguised as a paanan carrying these musical instruments and my bundle on a kavadi pole. To some soldiers who stopped me, I presented myself as a wandering paanan. They were fixed on capturing the king, of course, and that made it possible for me to get away without talking much.

It was only after I had covered quite some distance did it strike me that I had not taken even a second look at Ezhimala, which had given me so much.

I roamed in the neighbouring lands for a while. Then my love for the sea took me to the parathavar and the umanar, and I lived among them for some time. Some of them knew that I was an important member of the king's inner circle and took good care of me.

My days passed thus, until wandering paanar brought the news of Nannan's death. That worried me. If I came to be revealed as someone who once had Nannan's ear, I was not likely to be spared. The Chera king's spies were everywhere. For the same reason, the chieftains of the lands nearby would cast me out, or take my head, actually, for all the cruelty wreaked on them by Nannan's army in war. It was wiser for me to move to some distant land.

Once again, I became a wanderer with no fixed destination. I pretended to be a paanan and travelled through many lands. The musical instruments felt utterly alien to me – it was as though I was carrying something that was not mine. I begged for food from houses and slept in public inns and stone pavilions. Then I walked along the seashore and the rivers. Somewhere along the way, I managed to get on a merchant boat that was returning after selling goods. I reached Kuttanaad.

I had heard that our ancestors hailed from there. A land where the waters flowed under patches of luxuriant foliage. A land of ponds and lakes and rivers, and canals and fields beside them. Many people there were parathavar, who caught fish. Their little huts dotted the landscape. Some of the larger houses that I saw probably belonged to merchants. Many kinds of boats filled the waterways. The merchants took heaps of pepper to Purakkaad, which was near, and Muchiri, which was far, on their canoes hollowed out of single logs of wood. Perhaps they returned with heaps of gold! I went eastwards from there. As I moved further east, the watery landscape receded.

On the hill slopes, lush pepper vines climbed the tall trees. Bunches of pepper, round and shiny, like green pearls. I corrected myself: this is the land in which the water spreads below and the trees thrive above. Where were the paana huts here? Were any of our kin still here? I did not feel compelled to find them. Even in a land where they harvest pure gold, the paanar will do nothing but sing and dance for a living! I had contemplated spending some time there, but then decided against it. What if hanging around in Chera lands landed me in danger?

I left Kuttanaad and took the routes that led south-east. I crossed the Pamba on a ferry boat and climbed the hills. I was beginning to tire of walking on forest paths. I sated my hunger and thirst eating fruit plucked from the trees and drinking from ponds. The forest was full of monkeys and peacocks. It seemed that there were leopards deep in it. I also heard the trumpeting of elephants. There must be many traps set for them around! I am a lone tusker. Where lies the trap set for me? I could not afford a single misstep. I would rather lie down and die than stumble into a trap, I told myself. I pulled myself up, raised my head, bolstered my pride, quickened my pace and soon got out of the jungle. After some days, I reached Pothiyilmala.

This was Ay Eyinan's land. The image of his corpse lying on the battlefield shielded from the sun by the flapping wings of birds high in the air above rose in my mind. I sat down, looking briefly at the birds roosting in the clumps of trees around. Were they chirping 'eyi-nan, eyi-nan'? Were they telling each other that Eyinan's enemy had arrived? My dear birds, Mayilan has neither foe nor friend! His dearest wish is to stay alone even when it may seem that he lives among people as one of them.

The streets were not very busy. It was noon but the mist still hung in the air. A faint chill caressed my body. When I felt that it was spreading inside too, I stopped by the wayside for a few moments and closed my eyes. A commotion nearby made me open them. People were running away frantically! I kept away from the chaos as much as I could. An elephant, apparently, was running wild. It was a gift received by a group of paanar. They were running after it, unable to control it. But as it was in a violent mood, they shrank from it too! That was amusing. What to do if you could not control that which you got as a gift! The thought of their plight made me laugh again and again.

I felt wary of approaching the chieftain who ruled Pothiyilmala. This was Eyinan's territory. Even the birds may betray me. I chose to stay in a village rather removed from both the Ay lands that belonged to him and the other local chiefdoms. It was a place through which the road to neighbouring lands passed. It was there that a crucial meeting took place, by chance.

I was resting at a public inn, lying down with my bundle as a pillow. I was tired and soon fell asleep – only to be roused rudely by a sudden, painful jab. I jumped up with a shriek. It was a soldier. Uncontrolled anger made me charge at him, and I slapped him hard on the cheek. He probably did not expect such a furious response. He tried to come at me with his bow, but I blocked his blows. Soon, it turned into a fistfight.

'Why did you hurt me?' I yelled at him.

'Why didn't you wake up when I shook you? This place is meant for soldiers to rest!'

'You soldiers ought to be kind to the poor! It is your king who is shamed by your violence!'

'So even beggars are now beginning to bargain? This shouldn't be answered with words!'

He freed himself and delivered a mighty punch. I crashed to the ground.

'What requires a verbal response can be dealt with just that alone!'

I did not give up, even though I was floored.

'For the strong, their strength. For the rich, their coin. But the strength and wealth of the ignorant are a greater danger than the poverty of the wise!'

That made him stop. Then, he helped me up. I tried to pull myself away, but it was useless. To my great surprise, he began to wipe off the dirt from my body.

'Come,' he said. 'I have something to propose.'

I was still suspicious, but he grabbed my hand and took me out of the inn. I felt my anger ebb, and so I followed him.

'I sense that you are no ordinary beggar. Can you tell me who you are and what your situation is?'

'After such a skirmish?'

I was in pain. I gritted my teeth and swallowed it.

'Are you in hiding?'

Now, that gave me a real shock.

'No, I am a wanderer. I go from land to land seeking my keep. Yes, I am a beggar.'

'I know that is not true. Let me tell you about myself. I am Makeeran. I come from the Chera lands. I am here to meet the Vel of Ay.'

I didn't respond.

'Not ready to talk, eh? Never mind! Do you want to come with me?'

I held myself back from an answer. He was waiting for one. Well, I was sick of lugging myself from one place to another disguised as a beggar. What do I care who this is? For he who has nothing to lose, anything in hand is a gain! I decided that I would tell him more about myself only after I got to know him better.

Seeing me take my time, he went back into the inn. I followed him.

'Wherever you are going, I am coming too.'

Makeeran smiled knowingly. As though he was sure I would make that choice.

'Rest well today. We shall leave together tomorrow.'

We set out the next day. Besides Makeeran, there were four mounted soldiers. I clambered up behind one of them on his horse. The horses trotted on through the plains and crossed the river on the ferry. When night began to fall, we reached a band of maravar. All of a sudden, my memories swallowed me. It was as though all the knowledge that I had acquired later was peeling away. The callousness that had hardened within me as a boy once again protruded into my heart.

'You are perplexed, aren't you?'

'Not at all.'

Makeeran laughed aloud, hearing my reply.

'In that case, let me tell you something.'

He made sure that no one was around, and began to speak.

'I was sure after our meeting that we can work together. This is work that needs knowledge, shrewdness and a fearless mind! If your step fails you, you are dead. But if you are clever, you will be covered in gold and gifts.'

I got the drift but remained silent, pretending to be puzzled.

'I told you that we are Chera warriors, but that isn't completely true. I am one of the generals of the king of Thakadur, Athiyaman Neduman Anchi. I also join the marava bands sometimes! There are some secret tasks to be carried out for the king. I want to know if you can work for us.'

'Stopping beating around the bush,' I barked. 'You want me to spy for you? Who are you a spy for? The Cheras or Thakadur? Or are you a spy for both, a double-crosser on both sides?'

'You know well that we don't reveal such details. Even if I offer to, it may not be the truth. But I can tell you this much: we work for the Cheras. Or, to be precise, for the Mighty Three. Two vassals have been more than a headache for the Cheras – Thakadur, ruled by Athiyaman Neduman Anchi, and Parambunaad, ruled by Vel Paari. It will not be easy to subdue these chieftains, and so we must conspire. Hence the need for spies.'

'I know the Arichiyal like the palm of my hand. I understand.'

'That I sensed when we were arguing!' Makeeran smiled. 'I will tell you what you must do. You must go to Parambumala without delay. I will go to Thakadur. I will tell you everything in detail in good time. There's one thing you need to know right now. The Chera king's word must be obeyed to the letter. Never forget, we are the pawns in this game.'

'That too I know very well.'

'Tell me at least now who you are.'

'What if I lie to you?'

'You probably know what happens to disloyal spies. Should I tell you?'

I laughed out loud. Then I told him everything, from how I left home early in life until the happenings at Ezhimala. I was sure that it was better to tell him everything, for everything hidden would be dragged out into the open sometime or the other. I knew that I must have been spotted by spies during my wanderings.

Makeeran and two others left for Vanchi that very day. He had told me that he would go to Thakadur from there and would be late to return. I stayed with the maravar band. I did not join in their raids; even if I wanted to, I could not. I had changed too much since the old days. But the maravar took really good care of me and I did not go anywhere else. Some days passed. Makeeran did not return, but two of his comrades came.

Things are moving as planned, they told me: 'The Mighty Three are going to meet soon. You must go there. Makeeran will tell you about what needs to be done when you reach.'

I nodded. I was not afraid. On the contrary, the challenge felt exhilarating. The following day, I rode pillion with one of the soldiers and we were off. It was a day's journey, to a place on the borders of the Chera kingdom. We reached a tent atop a hill, heavily guarded. One of the soldiers who rode with us went into the darkness behind the tent and fetched Makeeran.

'The Mighty Three are inside, holding talks,' he said. 'Only when the meeting is over will we know what our tasks are.'

We waited. After the royal conference was over, Makeeran went back behind the tent. I had to wait a very long time for him to return. He came back and gave me a quick summary of what I was expected to do.

As we were conferring, an old woman came out of the tent. Makeeran took me to her.

'That's Avvaiyar. It is useful for you to know her. She lives in Athiyaman Neduman Anchi's palace. She is close to the king. She has sung many songs about him,' Makeeran informed me as we walked towards her. 'Don't dish out to her anything to do with your earlier life . . .'

We were now with her. Makeeran introduced me.

'Avva, this is a friend of mine. A knowledgeable fellow, smart too! But what to say, he is still bitten by the wander bug!'

Avvaiyar gave me a kindly smile. The smile wiped away the wrinkles on her cheek, and she looked younger. 'That's how it is. Knowledge and riches don't go together.'

'He was born a paanan. His kin are still back home. I saw him hanging around like a beggar, and so got him to come with me.'

'That's good! Our king is kind even to beggars. And to paanans, of course, no need to say!'

'That was my thought too, Avva. But he wants to go to Parambumala.'

'Vel Paari is a generous hero, too. I too have sung of him – as he who bestows tuskers, the size of hills, and many more valuable things, on even beggars! But I hear that his wealth has dwindled . . .'

'I am not fascinated by wealth,' I cut in. 'I seek knowledge.'

Avvaiyar looked approving. 'That is appropriate,' she said. 'But why go to Parambumala for it?'

'Is it not the place where the great poet Kapilar lives? Famed as he is for his verses, he is also known to be a great scholar in many streams of knowledge. I want to see him. And find out if I can learn more from him.'

Makeeran looked truly amazed now.

'You are right,' Avvaiyar said. 'Meet Kapilar. Only good will come to you!'

She placed her hands on my head, blessing me.

When we were walking back, Makeeran laughed, patting me on the back.

'Avvaiyar is such an important person – she is often the king's emissary. She's here in that capacity. I just

238

thought it might be useful for us that you meet her . . . but you outdid yourself!'

'I didn't tell her anything other than what you were already telling her.'

'True, I told her about your going to Parambumala, but the reasons that you set forth to her! I was truly amazed! You *are* a shrewd one indeed! Just right for this work!' Makeeran hugged me.

Before long, I was on my way to Parambumala.

Six

The best way to cosy up to Vel Paari was through Kapilar. But I was not sure how to make my way into his circle. Better not mention the name Mayilan. It was quite likely that people who knew me from Nannan's court were here. Because I was close to the king, the spies here might have reported about me too. Kapilar was very close to Paranar. If they met sometime, then it was very likely that all my trickeries would be revealed. But I looked very different now, though. My beard and hair had grown out. But I must change my name. I chose another name as I walked. I found one. Chami.

'Chami . . .'

I called out the name to myself. As I walked, I kept calling myself by that name, telling myself that I was fooling everyone else. It might take quite some time to fool my own self! Till then, I needed to be alert.

As soon as I reached Parambunaad, I went to meet Kapilar. He was of a serious mien. I held myself back a bit. Approaching him with visible humility, I told him that I came from the Chera lands and was a seeker of knowledge. Kapilar must have been a bit impressed, seeing that I could read and write well and that my knowledge of Arichiyal was not negligible. I begged him for a place to stay for some days. He was close to the king, so everything was easy.

There were other ways to become close to Kapilar. I became his scribe, writing down his songs on palm-leaf pages. Children came there to learn their letters. I became their teacher. I was careful to dust his collection of manuscripts and eager to ask questions: this pleased him.

There was music and dance in the palace every day. When the noise became rather irritating, I showed my frustration.

'Is it like this there every day? How can dance and music be enjoyable when it is served day and night?'

Kapilar smiled.

'That is Vel Paari! A hero in war. Valiant! But his love is not for war, it is for song and dance. He never refuses a hand that stretches out to him for a favour. I have felt that his generosity tilts towards those in need, and especially the paanar. The dance and music are only excuses.'

'Yes. Master, you are well-versed in the art of ruling. Tell me, is such generosity commendable? Does it bode well for a ruler?'

'Chami, if you think of it that way, no. But I, who have partaken of such generosity, how can I deny it?'

'Well, all of us don't think that way. Gifts must be given to those who are worthy of them. And given with an eye on the store of wealth one possesses!'

Kapilar was silent.

'Master, are you not close to the king? Can't you tell him this?'

'I have,' said Kapilar. 'But his only response, always, is a smile.'

'I fear that this will end in the ruin of this land!'

Did Kapilar wince? Did he suspect me?

'Chami, I too share your fear . . .' he said. 'This chiefdom once had three hundred villages under it. Now all that's left is this hill and town.'

That was a relief! I had worried for nothing!

It looked like everything would work out the way I wanted it to. Anyway, we did not take up this subject later.

The next step was crucial, and I had to be very careful working it out. I spent some days trying to figure out how exactly I could accomplish what I had been sent to do. Meanwhile, one of Makeeran's comrades paid a visit. I gave him a report.

'We are halfway there. Excellent progress. No need to wait any more.' This was the message Makeeran sent through him.

I agreed. 'But I need protection,' I insisted. 'If something happens to me.'

'Rest assured! It is not just the Chera armies, but also those of the other two kings have taken their positions around Parambumala. And not just for your protection. You are the thread that connects a number of key points in an elaborate trap. I will be here when it is time.'

The messenger left. I was now clear about what needed to be done. I would speak to Kapilar without delay.

One evening, when the sounds of dancing and music seemed to be soaring sky-high like never before, I went to him.

'Master, please be patient with me. I must speak with you.'

'What is this preface for? You may speak.'

'What I say may anger you. Please think carefully, and you will be convinced that I am right. My heart tells me that all this singing and dancing is going to wreck this land.'

'That is something you have been saying all this while! Why bring it up now?'

'I hear that the Mighty Three are likely to move their armies to conquer Parambumala.'

'How did you know?'

'Someone who came from the Chera lands hinted at something like that to me.'

'Why should they tell you such things? The king has special people to attend to such matters.'

'I am one of them. But I am your man too. Vel Paari must be protected. I am seeking your help.'

'Chami, who are you?' Kapilar flew into a rage. 'A spy! Is it not true? This is treason!'

'You can say that I am a spy. But I am not a traitor. I am loyal to you and Paari.'

'Get away from me! No – that will not do. You must be shackled and imprisoned or killed! Let the king decide!'

'Please, you who know Arichiyal so well must not indulge in such an outburst. Irrespective of whether you and I side with the king, the Mighty Three will achieve their aim.'

'No. Vel Paari cannot be defeated.'

'That is an illusion. The powerful Vel does not exist any more. He has given away all his wealth and his foes know this weakness well.'

Kapilar clapped his hands to summon his attendant.

'Do not behave unwisely. The Mighty Three have surrounded this land. The king himself cannot harm me now. It is possible that Vel Paari may be murdered by the time you drag me to him! We must at least protect the king's life. You must help me in that.'

When he heard my low-pitched words, Kapilar sank down to the ground in alarm, his hand on his head.

'Why do you worry?' I continued. 'If the two of us can work together, then we can at least save the king's life. If we delay, even that may be impossible. You know perfectly well that the king cannot stand a combined assault by the Mighty Three. Haven't you yourself composed verses about lands ravaged by war? Do I need to describe the desecration to you? Should we just stand watching while Paari is killed and the land devastated?'

I said that in a single breath.

'You are cleverer than you need to be. I thought you were learned, and that you wanted to learn more. When a killer elephant is released into the bathing ghat, people are warned by the beating of drums! But I received no such warning about you! You came in so quietly, I took you in, not seeing you for a spy. Ah! Though unwittingly, I have betrayed Paari, my dearest friend!'

'Master, you are half right and half wrong. The Mighty Three would like to avoid bloodshed in this conquest. But if that is impossible, they will not hesitate to shed blood. That will happen, whether we are with him or not. But if you will work with me, we can save the king and the land. That is what I am trying to suggest. This is not betrayal.'

'What do you suggest?'

'I don't know all of it, but let me tell you what I know. They intend to take a route that you yourself have suggested in some of your songs. You know well enough that if people come seeking his largesse with dance and music, he will yield anything. That is precisely what they want to exploit.'

'All this they can do on their own. Why do they need me?'

'Master, you are wise. Among the wordsmiths of the world today, you are the best. They need someone like that. Mighty kings crave fame! Killing Paari, known as Vellal for his great generosity, can only bring them infamy. They want to make sure that their deeds do not bring them disrepute. All these are the reasons why they want to approach Paari's bosom friend. Your words have great value. And besides, you are an anthanan! The Chera king Chelvakkadumko Vaazhiyaathan does not bow to anyone but the anthanar! That mighty ruler believes that this must be achieved without attracting censure from you.'

Kapilar listened silently. He thought for a long time. Then, as if he had taken a decision, he said, 'This land, which I love so much, should not suffer. Paari should not die. I will help.'

I touched his feet reverentially.

'Paanar and koothar arrive here daily. Some of the soldiers of the armies of the Mighty Three will be among them. They will choose a day that suits them.'

Before I left, I also cautioned him.

'If Vel Paari or anyone else gets to know about this, things will go awry. Remember, in that case, the land is sure to be conquered! The Three will think about fame and name only after that. I will find out what is next and be back.'

I was impatient for Makeeran's comrade to return. He came, and I told him about Kapilar's change of mind. He was eager to report it. I got to know from him that many of the palace guards had been persuaded to join us. He went out and came back again, and I went back to Kapilar.

'Now things are going to unfold quickly. When you go to meet the king, please check around the palace well.'

Kapilar merely hummed. He then left to meet the king, as usual.

I waited there. There was some movement outside, but I did not pay attention. The regular crowd that came to see him, I thought.

Kapilar returned after some time.

'Some people are waiting outside. Paanar and koothar, probably. Let me deal with them.'

When Kapilar returned, I had already drawn up a plan.

'Did you say they were paanar and koothar? Have you dismissed them?'

'They were sent here by someone dear to me, my friend Paranar. I have sent them off to the rest house.'

'Excellent. We need them.'

'No. They cannot be involved in any conspiracy. Paranar sent them to me.'

'So what? There's no time to lose. Let them stay here for some days. In the meantime, we can think carefully and decide.'

Before Kapilar could say a word, I got up to leave. The paanar and koothar had not left yet. It was quite dark, so I could not take a good look at them. I did not wait to observe them; I walked away. Makeeran's men were expecting me.

Seven

The momentous hour had finally arrived. I spoke with Kapilar and fixed everything according to the instructions that Makeeran's men brought. This was playing with fire, truly. Anything could happen. And what would survive in the end? One could not say. My heart pounded, like the beats of the neythal para. I collected my thoughts and once again went over the steps of the plan.

I reached the palace before the paanar and koothar. The soldiers who Makeeran's people had lured into the conspiracy let me in; I mingled with them. Vel Paari entered amidst the din of songs of praise. Everyone kept standing until he sat on the throne.

But isn't this the last time you'll mount it . . .

I snuffed out the faint anguish that sparked within me.

Some petitioners approached him, and some beggars and individual songsters appeared before him. The king settled their issues one by one. Then, a group of paanar and koothar accompanied by Kapilar's attendant Pengan came in. I was now doubly alert. I checked if the others were in the positions assigned to them.

It was then that my eyes fell on the group that had entered with Pengan. A single look, and my head began to ache splittingly. Achan and Amma! My siblings! Perumpaanan too!

It was devastating. Unbearable. Tears pricked my eyes and I now wept out of sheer desperation.

How did I miss them at Kapilar's house? Alas, they are going to be embroiled in this bloodbath! If only they were spared in the mayhem! I covered my face with my hands, moved away behind the soldiers, and hid from my kin.

It was not deliberate, but I had made pawns of my own people in the game I was part of! I could only stand there – helpless, forlorn, guilty, bewildered – holding the severed thread of a kite that was already lost.

The singing and dancing got over somehow. Then the king asked them what gifts they desired. Exactly as planned, three men belonging to the clans of the

Mighty Three stepped up from among the paanar and koothar and declared that they desired the land itself. We had reckoned that the king would give in, seeing that he had no way out.

But Paari drew his sword and leapt forward. For a moment it was as if I had turned to stone, but the next moment, I drew my sword, went behind Paari, slit his throat and sprinted away before his guards could surround me. I knew that I would be pursued. Pushing my way through the crowd, I got ahead of my pursuers. I slipped away from a swordsman who came at me, and someone else took the hit. A massive crowd had gathered outside the palace. I plunged into it and disappeared. Then I made my way out of the crowd and was going to sneak away . . . it was only then that I noticed the man who had taken the sword meant for me.

Achan! I stopped in my tracks. He had fallen! I thought I had screamed, but my voice did not come out at all. I was petrified for a moment, a cold pillar of stone. Then, sensing that my pursuers had spotted me, I darted off again, leaping over Achan's fallen body. I kept looking back even when I reached my co-conspirators, who were waiting outside. I could not return; all I could do was accompany them. I cried openly, loudly. That was very rare for me. Achan! Achan! I kept mumbling as we rode away.

Our comrades were waiting with horses at a distance.

'The paanar and koothar who were there today are my kin. Please ensure their safe passage.' I told them.

'We cannot do anything that wasn't planned and fixed before.'

I begged them. They would not budge.

'I am not coming if they can't come along.'

'Don't be a fool! If you stay back you are dead! They have committed no crime, they will be spared. If Paari's warriors get to know that they are your blood, they will slay them all for sure.'

They were not going to yield. I could see no other way. Even as I got away from Parambumala with them, I struggled to control my feelings. I covered my mouth and eyes with my hands to stop my sobs and tears.

We reached the territory of the maravars. Makeeran was waiting.

'Everything went excellently!'

He patted me on the pack. I clapped my hands on my face and wailed.

I was back again among the maravar. I had to stay with them for a long period. Makeeran was busy travelling between Vanchi and Thakadur. From those of us who returned from Parambumala, I got to know that Achan had died and my people had left the place. I could not cure myself of the numbness in my nerves. I was stricken by terrible sorrow and bottomless fear.

My people were wandering through unknown lands without Achan. The look in Achan's eyes as he lay wounded and dying haunted me day and night.

'My people are out there alone, and they know nothing about the world. I have only added to their pain by causing my father's death. I have done nothing for my mother and siblings. I cannot join them ever. You know my state – I beg you, please stand with them and look after them like they were your own!' I begged Makeeran when he came back.

'Each one of us writes our own fate! Let it be. Calm down. I will do whatever is necessary for them. I will find them wherever they may have gone. I will personally make sure that they have whatever they need. Do not worry.'

Makeeran kept going away and coming back. I learned from him that he had found my kin and that they lived quite well. Once, when he came back from Vanchi, he came to me with a booming laugh.

'Did you know? Kapilar is now the Chera king's right-hand man! When I went to meet him he was sitting with Kapilar and stroking his palm. Why is this hand so soft, the king asked. And Kapilar's response! He said his hands, which were good only for making balls of rice and rich meat curry tempered with mustard and eating them, could not be compared with the king's hands, which wielded the staff that tamed the elephant, held the reins that controlled the horse, dispatched arrows from bows and endlessly bestowed gifts on others! He has also made many other songs of praise. In return the king has settled on him all the land that was visible from the top of a hill! That is exactly how wordsmiths ought to be – excellent schemers!'

His laughter dripped with derision. I could join in it outwardly, but inwardly I could not.

'But then, why are we, who won a whole chiefdom for the king, still condemned to stay with this marava band?'

'That will change. Be patient for some more time. It is best that you stay here. We may have finished the job in Parambumala, but there remains much to be done in Thakadur and Vanchi. I will be busy with all that.'

Makeeran left. I continued to stay with the maravar, but that life was getting hard to bear. I did not wish to get closer to anyone. There was no question of joining the marauders on their raids. I had set out in life aiming to achieve much, though I did not know what. My inner world was now raging and seething. All sorts of different things were whizzing, swirling and tossing about in there wildly – song and dance, learning and looting, law and massacre . . . I began to feel that my end was going to be like that of a hunting dog torn to pieces by its prey. I needed to run away somewhere. I must find Makeeran and ask for a proper reward for the work that I had done for him. There would be no life otherwise.

Makeeran did not return for a long time. I began to worry. I had no news of my kin, either. I began to spend more and more time alone. The members of the marava band were also isolating me, I noticed. I decided to risk it and question one of Makeeran's closest mates.

'Where is Makeeran? Why haven't I heard from him for so long?'

He tried to avoid the question and looked flustered; I caught hold of him and repeated the question. In the end, he blurted out: 'Please don't be angry with me. He's been wooing your sister. I heard that they live together now.'

I was struck dumb. So this was what he meant when he said that he would take care of my folk! Was he duping them? He was a spy. He could not be trusted.

That troubled me for some time. But when I thought more about it, I began to see no fault in it. From whatever I had seen of him till then, Makeeran was loyal to me. He was not deceiving my sister. After all, he was living with her.

'Why should I be angered by this? Makeeran is strong and capable. If he had mentioned it to me, I would have stood by him. Where are they now?'

The man did not give a clear answer.

'I don't know. Probably in Thakadur or Muchiri. I learned this from our other mates. Makeeran never reveals anything about himself.'

'Let it be. You told me at least this much! What is happening in Muchiri?'

'The Chera king has been staying there for some time now. Makeeran may be there, but he could also be in Thakadur.'

'I am sick of this place. I want to leave.'

'Where will you go?'

'Not sure where. Somewhere!'

So I prepared to depart. The maravar tried to stop me. I could not make out if it was because they had grown fond of me, or because they feared that I could not be trusted.

'You may leave if you wish. If you tell us where you want to go, we can take you there.'

'If you can, get me past these paala wilds. I can carry on by myself from there. I intend to go to Muchiri.'

A gust of cool breeze comforted me when I got out of the barren wastes. To Muchiri! A joyful sea seemed to be lapping at my heart! Why not hop on one of the ships that docked there and sail away to some foreign land, I asked myself. My journey this time was very leisurely. This seemed a continuation of the long journeys on foot that had been my lot since I left Ezhimala.

The path I took ran over the plains. The trees were in full bloom. Birds played in them and cooed like little children. It was early summer. The town of Muchiri was on the banks of a river. Most people on the streets looked quite prosperous.

There was no certainty that Makeeran was there. He could be in Thakadur, but he was said to visit this town often. So I decided to stay until I met him. And to sketch a course of action for the future after that.

Better not go to the king. Would Kapilar be there? They say that he has become close to the king. Won't we have to meet someday? What would he say if we met? Kapilar, whom I had to bring around to our plan with so much persuasion, was now in the king's inner circle! And I, who paved the way for it all, was out on the streets! I was livid. To ease the irritation which grew steadily, I went to the seashore. This was a habit I had acquired at Ezhimala. Watching the waves lapping at the shore always calmed me down a little.

The shore was crowded that day. The parathavar's canoes were on the beach and on the waves. The brave fisherfolk ventured into the high seas to catch the chira fish. Their nets opened their wings in the air slowly, like large sea birds, fell upon the sea and dropped into its depths. Rows of drying fish dotted the beach. The umanar's salt pans glinted under the sun. And so many different people! Many from lands far away. Of many colours. Of many tongues. All of them must be camping somewhere close by. There were specific streets where they stayed, those of them who spent a long time in Muchiri.

They say that the yavanas have a temple of their own here. You'd want to keep looking at them – such interesting ways they have. So many ships, near and far, bobbing on the waves! I felt again the urge to get on one of them and leave for some distant land. I stood there for a long time, trying to picture myself standing under the high mast of a ship, taking in the sight of the sea that surrounded me.

Eight

I still wanted to know what went on in the king's camp; I still craved news from the royal inner quarters. But I could not go there. Anyway, there was no point in me going there without Makeeran. It seemed that no one in Muchiri knew me. That lifted a weight off my mind. That Makeeran had not turned up for so long worried me, though. He must be in Thakadur. I had to somehow stay on in this town till he returned.

I spent a lot of time on the seashore and begged for food at the homes of the fisherfolk. No home refused me a meal. When it was dark, I would lie down on some rock, my eyes on the light from some wayside lamp. I would listen to the hum of the sea. The busy chatter of people when ships docked. On the days of the vizhaavu festival, I could hear the women of the fisherfolk dance the kuravakkoothu. When I was in a dark place, I longed for light. When alone, I craved the company of people.

Sometimes I would walk through the streets of the town taking in the sights. I was wonderstruck by how the yavanas hurried to their ships with huge bundles full of pepper. I knew from my earlier journeys on foot that it came mostly from Kuttanaad. These people from faraway lands were taking the bundles of pepper on canoes to the large seafaring ships anchored farther away on the sea. What was their fascination with this spicy little seed?

I had made walking around the king's camp a regular habit. There was no way to find out if Makeeran had arrived. One day, I was walking on a street when the sight of a young chap coming up from the opposite direction made me catch my breath in alarm. He must have noticed me too. When he drew closer, I knew who he was. It was Chanthan, my playmate from childhood!

Before I could make a move, he was by my side. Though he shouted out my name, my reaction was to shrink away.

'We searched for you everywhere!'

He hugged me. It was no use pretending not to know him, because he clearly had no doubts at all as to who I was.

'How did you reach this place?'

My amazement broke through my chilly exterior.

'I came in search of you.'

'How did you know that I am here?'

'I guessed.'

Chanthan described how he had gone to Ezhimala and Parambumala and how our people had come to Muchiri when Chithira left them. I could only acknowledge his words; I could not reply to anything. When I heard that all our kin were here, I became desperate that there was nowhere I could run to and hide. But I did not show it.

'Mayila, I know that you have many secrets . . . you hide much. Here, in the palace, they found out that we are your kin and stopped us from meeting the king.'

'How can that be? No one here knows me!'

'I am certain — they stopped us mentioning your name. You must find a way for us to meet the king, though. Let's go to our people.'

I tried to free my arm from his firm grip.

'Let's meet later.'

'No! You will disappear if I let you go!'

I summoned all my strength, twisted free my arm, and took to my heels as fast as I could.

He ran after me. 'Do not come near! I don't want to see anyone!' I shouted as I ran.

Chanthan was persistent; he caught hold of me again. I resisted him with all my strength. We grappled and fell to the ground. A crowd gathered to watch. I escaped into the crowd, pushing the spectators aside and running through obscure alleys. I got away from him. I ducked behind a gigantic tree.

What was happening? Why were my people being stopped?

I had led my kin into some trap. Someone had been pursuing me and them, all this time. Shaken and sad I had been, but now fearful too. There was no sign of Makeeran. Now was the time to lie low, far from any prying eyes. And find out what I needed to know.

I continued to live on the seashore for some more days and drew closer to some of the yavanas I met there. Though we could not understand each other's tongues, I got a fair idea of their lands and ways. My longing to get on a ship and sail away grew stronger.

At the end of a long wait, I finally ran into Makeeran. We saw each other on the street; immediately, we moved to a secluded corner. He claimed that he had been searching for me. Anyway, here was a chance to at least find out what was going on. And end my days on the seashore. But when I tried to accompany him, Makeeran refused to take me with him.

'I have other things to do here. You cannot stay with me. I will make other arrangements.'

'Is Chithira with you?'

'No, she is in Thakadur.'

'There's something I need to know right now. Who is preventing my people from meeting the king?'

Makeeran looked stumped. That made me more indignant.

'Are you the reason that they were turned away?'

'No, I knew that they were coming here, but I did not meet them. I have some people among the palace guards. I will try to find out from them.'

Without much delay, Makeeran found me a house quite close to the seashore. The pulse of the waves made the tide rise and fall inside my mind. When I closed my eyes, I saw ships. I heard many tongues. Even in my sleep I found myself alone on the sea.

Makeeran visited again and told me: 'Seems it is Kapilar who's been sabotaging your people's chances. The guards won't reveal it. But it's certain that someone very close to the king has played a role.'

'Is Kapilar in Muchiri?'

'Yes. I haven't spoken to him directly. And he doesn't really know me. But I have seen him here frequently with the king.'

I thought about it. Time to confront Kapilar!

Makeeran pointed out his dwelling. I did not feel like biding my time and so walked straight in. He was sitting on the floor, scribbling something. Must be a new song about the Chera king's splendour.

I thought he would leap up when he saw me. That did not happen. He merely squinted at me.

'I knew that you would come here.'

'Yes. I had to come.'

'What do you want?'

'I need to know a few things.'

Kapilar frowned.

'My kin have been stopped from meeting the king. Who is doing this?'

'Oh, so they are your people! That you did not say!'

'I did not know then. It was too late when I got to know. How did you learn of it, master?'

'I am not idling in the lands of the Cheras! I found out what happened in Parambunaad . . . from some of your co-conspirators. I pieced together their accounts to get a sense of what had really happened that day.'

'Let it be . . . but you have not given me a reply.'

'Yes, it is I who prevented them from entering.'

'Why?'

'Don't I know what you did back in Parambumala? I know that you are here with more such vile aims! They are after all the kin of a traitor like you. I should of course stop you from prying . . . if you try any tricks . . .'

'Traitor? If anyone was a traitor in this game, it was you, master!'

'Each deed of yours – after you joined me under the false name of Chami – was false. It is you who used me! Turned me into a filthy accomplice! And you dare to call *me* a traitor?'

'It is true that it is I who came to you and made an arrangement. But it is you who wished for Paari's destruction!'

'Me? Who do you think you are? Get out this instant!' he cried.

'Don't think you can frighten me! I too have some things to say!'

'I will not listen!'

'You must! I am a spy. You are a scholar who knows well the art of spying, you know how spies behave. I don't have to tell you. A spy does not decide anything; he merely obeys orders and does his best. He is just a leather puppet in the hands of kings and their trusted advisers. He is loyal only to them. But you are not like that. Vel Paari trusted you blindly. He gave you everything you needed. What did you do in return?'

'Traitor! You played me with your words and now you are doing a somersault? Was it not you who manipulated me like a puppet? I became your accomplice in the hope that the land and its ruler would be safeguarded. Then you butchered that fount of generosity, the Vellal! Parambumala was reduced to a ball of rice trampled by an elephant!'

'It is not my mind that has changed, it is yours. True, it is I who killed Vel Paari's body. But you had already murdered him inwardly.'

'*I* . . . ?'

'Yes. You, indeed. Let me say more. The Mighty Three had learned long before I came to you how Paari could be felled. By listening to your songs.'

Kapilar did not seem unsettled outwardly, but I could see him cringe inwardly.

'It is you who let them know that Paari cannot be defeated with an army, but if the paanar and koothar came and begged, they would win the land itself! And just like you suggested, they used pawns like us to get what they wanted. It is we who lost . . . me and my kin . . . and it is you who won.'

When I saw Kapilar grow agitated, everything that I had suppressed till then broke free and erupted.

'When it became evident that Paari did not have much more to give, you collaborated to destroy him. When you learned that the Chera king was in awe of anthanar, you migrated here! How come the king here places so much trust in those who are so opportunistic? Maybe one could say that this is your habit. And what did you do to my starving kin? They have been hauling themselves through the land, unable to even find food. You blew up their last refuge! Great poet, indeed! You have received all the land that can be seen from a hilltop for singing praises of the Chera king! But it will not last! What you did to Vel Paari who loved and trusted you will wipe away all that you gain!'

Kapilar sat hunched, his head bowed. Was he weeping? Seeing that gave me a boost. I lost all scruple.

'I will not spare you! Even a spy stays loyal to his kin. But you and the songs that you sang provided the key for the defeat of the friend who loved you the most. Let the fame of the great poet who betrayed his own words spread in the land!'

I stamped hard on the floor and marched out. Before getting out of the yard, I spat on it sneeringly.

I must go away. There was no question of joining my people. I must find Makeeran. Settle the reward for the task well done. I walked briskly. I did not know where he stayed. Anyway, it was not wise to go there. I went back home.

The days rolled on. I did see Makeeran in between, but he did not say a word about what was due to me. I had helped him grab a whole kingdom! What cause to delay my reward now? I did not feel like making a demand. He ought to have known that I deserved a reward, and richly so.

I was still staying in the house he had found me. His comrades brought me food every day. But that wouldn't do, would it? I was, after all, once a confidant of a king, a member of his inner circle! I had had enough of living like a tramp.

One day, Makeeran came to me all excited.

'Did you hear? Kapilar has gone away for good!'

'Really? Excellent!'

'And do you want to know what happened after that?'

'What?'

'Our friends from Parambumala told me this. He apparently gave up his life – while singing songs of Paari's glory!'

That terrible jolt left my mouth parched and bitter. I concealed it.

'But . . . why . . . ?' I stammered.

'I have no clue. But you met him, didn't you? What need then to seek a reason?'

Speech failed me. I tried to run away. Makeeran barred my way.

'The king is devastated. He hasn't learned yet that you are behind this. But if he does, that's not going to be good for you!'

I grabbed Makeeran's hand and held it tight. With an inward shudder, I realized that I too needed someone to lean upon in a moment of crisis. But Makeeran's hand felt weak and cold.

'So you two are friends!' A sudden interruption drew our attention away. 'I am going to end this game you are playing together today!'

Chanthan!

'Game? What game? What do you know to say such things?' Makeeran snapped at him.

'Yes, there is much I do not know. But I do know that all that has happened till now was a farce you two plotted together!'

We did not respond.

'Tell me, why did you abandon that girl who trusted you?'

Makeeran seemed to recoil. Suddenly, he was seeking a way out of the place.

'Which girl?'

Stupefied, I turned to Chanthan.

'Don't you dare say a word,' he spat at me. 'You, who did not have a care for your own sibling! This fellow has another woman here. He lives with her!'

Makeeran was going to make a dash for some bylane, but I grabbed his arm firmly.

'I did not know anything. What happened?' I asked Chanthan.

'You didn't know? Well, then. I don't know what things you tell each other. I stayed here though we could not meet the king – just to learn the truth. I have been following Makeeran since the day he came back here; he did not know that. I wanted to make sure that you knew of it, if you didn't already. And now, please get on with whatever charades you are planning together! We will no longer be your puppets!'

The moment Chanthan finished, I pounced on Makeeran.

'You shameless fellow!' I roared, 'Didn't I beg you to take care of my people? And this is what you did!'

Makeeran wrested his arm free.

'*Your people?* Really? You, who killed your own father, you dare to accuse me? You have no right!'

I had no answer. Chanthan looked petrified.

'It was not me . . . I didn't kill him . . .'

Chanthan walked away, not bothering to listen to my mumbling. Makeeran too walked away, completely unfazed. I could only watch them go.

Nine

When I finally sank down into the sand on the beach, a gale broke out inside me. It was simply not possible for me to carry on here any more. Nor could I go back to my kin. Once again, the desire to leave these lands overwhelmed me. Many are the lands in this world in which one may find great wealth. I must find the place with the brightest prospects.

It was with that intention that I tried to make connections with the yavanas. We communicated with our hands and faces. Soon, their words began to become more comprehensible. They would point to the big and small bundles of cinnamon and opium and pepper and try to converse. I could imagine the people who were waiting for these in some distant corners of the world. I walked through those lands filled with words that I could not comprehend. The peacocks that were to be sent to those faraway lands screamed in their cages. Kural, indeed! Funny, really, that our songsters glorify that screeching cry, calling it the sixth note!

The way these people coveted pepper would stump anyone. They claimed they used it to make their food tasty, to preserve meat and to make medicines. Not just pepper, they also sought cardamom and dried ginger, agarwood, sesame oil, ivory and rice! Also, pearls and gemstones and the areca nut that reached Muchiri from the eastern lands. I felt that I stood on the brink of a whole new world and new knowledge.

When I inquired if I could go with them, they smiled. I learned that if I went with them, I could return later as a guide. Through their gestures, they taught me about the role of the wind in sailing. I could even stay back if I did not wish to return. There were apparently many who did stay back. But it was the delight of the journey through the rolling waves that fascinated me.

I spent my time between the seashore and the house. On some days, I would take a walk by the banks of the Periyar. The air was not heavy with the pungent briny reek of the seashore; it was a gentle breeze that caressed the ripples lightly. One could hear the loud chatter of the washerwomen busy at work near the bathing places. Salt water was apparently good to get rid of dirt from clothes. On other days, I visited the lesser parts of the city and the neighbouring lands. Neither Chanthan nor Makeeran came in search of me.

Around this time, I was walking through a neighbouring settlement. There was some festival taking place in a temple; loud music could be heard. I was curious, and so I went there. It was the temple of Kannagi, who had torn out one of her breasts and flung it on the ground to burn down the city of Koodal. Whole crowds of possessed oracles were engaged in frenzied singing. Their loosened hair flew wild and danced to the rhythm of their sacred anklets. The vennikkoothu and the songs of the war bards began to roll in my mind. I wanted to join them, but I did not. I stood some distance away from the spectacle.

Suddenly – most unexpectedly – one of the oracles rushed at me. She was covered with blood that flowed down from her head. She neared me, her sword raised above her hair that flew wildly around, and with a roar that was filled with a kind of aggression that I had never seen before. Not knowing what that meant, I tarried there for a moment. The blade of the sword flashed like lightning above my head. Blood flowed from the deep gashes on my forehead and chest. I was thrown to the ground.

I was under the shade of a tree when I opened my eyes. The man applying salves on my wounds – I recognized him instantly – was none other than Perumpaanan! I tried to leap up, but my body would not move. Amma stood next to him, her head covered. I wanted to wipe her tears, but I could not move my hand. I had a vague memory of my younger brother who was standing next to her. Chanthan stood some distance away. But I shuddered in sheer horror when I noticed the little girl sitting near me. The same little girl who had rushed at me as the oracle! My little sister who had sung and danced in Vel Paari's palace that fateful day. I could not move. It was as if my head was frozen, cut off from my body.

'My child, please close your eyes. Please relax a little!'

I obeyed Perumpaanan. It was Amma who wiped the tears that flowed out of the corners of my eyes with the edge of her garment. The scent of that piece of cloth brought back the childhood that I had forgotten.

After some days, I was healed enough to sit up. Never once did I try to find out why the oracle had tried to hack me down. But Chanthan brought it up.

'Cheera has been like this for some time. You'd think she isn't in this world. Do you remember what happened at the temple?'

I recollected what had happened there. Then, slowly, I told them of all that had happened after I left home. Amma must have been weeping in her heart remembering Achan. But she did not show it. Would she be able to forgive me? I was a tree whose crown had broken when it was still young. If you can, please, pull me out by my roots, discard me!

When I was well enough to walk, Perumpaanan began to hasten preparations for us to leave Muchiri.

'Enough, no need to wander any more! No door has opened for us so far to help us escape our hardship, but at least we have found our Mayilan. Let us go back to our homeland.'

They were taking their revenge on me, repaying my venom with the soothing balm of tender love. But I was not strong enough to go off on my own, either.

We set off after a few days. I did not seek out Makeeran to bid him goodbye. His taunt about me being my father's killer still rang in my heart. I did not want his reward. The books say that there is no greater delight than hearing others praise one's son as learned and wise. But I, who took pride in my learning, what had I done? How would I make up for the injury? Even after so many days, I could still not find the courage to face Amma.

'Shouldn't we get Chithira? Won't she be alone?'

'She won't come. She's a proud one! Quite capable of being by herself.'

Chanthan described their visit to Thakadur. Deep respect for her resonated in his words. That was a surprise, but I did not reveal my feelings.

We went back taking the same paths through which I had run away from home. Each one of us seemed to be walking back through the same paths. My people were all with me, but all of them felt so far away! Each of us was absorbed in our own thoughts. We had achieved nothing. And the losses we had suffered were beyond compensation. Cheera had not yet uttered a single word to me. Did she harbour the desire to avenge our father's death? There was no way to find out.

After walking for a long time, we reached Aanamala. The tall peaks were covered with mist even during the day. A light rain was falling.

When the rock caves became visible through the vanishing tendrils of mist, Chanthan said, 'This is where we first met Paranar.'

We rested there for a little. But my memories and those of my kin of that place diverged, of course. We made haste to leave.

We had barely begun to walk again when someone hailed us from behind.

We turned. The form was still veiled in mist, but the voice was unforgettable – it was Paranar's!

A bolt of lightning cut through me. Who was dragging me back, again and again, to the paths that I once trod? I wanted to run away and hide somewhere, but my legs refused to move.

He walked towards us, and we towards him.

'We never expected to see you again here, lord!'

Perumpaanan said that with folded hands.

'I knew that you would return,' he said.

The others were bemused by that statement, but I knew exactly what he meant.

I reached his side in a single bound and fell at his feet. He pulled his foot away instantly.

'A moulting snake is still a snake . . .' I heard him whisper.

'Please forgive me!' Maybe no one noticed me burst into tears in the dark.

'Get up. I am not the one who should forgive you.'

I scrambled up.

'Let that be. Now, tell me, have you found the means to sustain yourselves?'

'No. We are returning home. We could not find refuge in any land.'

Perumpaanan's voice quivered in disillusionment.

'I knew that! That's why I waited here for you so long!'

My people could not see what he meant by that. Perumpaanan began to relate in detail all that had transpired during our wanderings and was soon immersed in his story. Paranar listened carefully.

'You need not live any more in such sorrow, like homeless people. This stretch of land, Umberkaadu, was granted to me by the king. You may settle down here.'

'No! Oh great poet, let us leave! We will go back to our homeland.'

'So, you want to wallow forever in distress?'

He sounded grave.

'I am telling you! I, who showed you the way! I am leaving this place. As long as kings demand songs of praise, poets need not worry about their keep. I am gifting you this land, Umberkaadu. Go to the rock cave where I lived. There are things there that I cannot carry on my journey. I give them to you.'

All of us, and Perumpaanan too, folded our hands in salutation and bowed. Paranar smiled, turned, and walked away, disappearing into the mist.

Overwhelmed, our emotions overflowing, sobbing, we lowered our bundles to the ground. After some time, we went into the cave. There was a very large bundle placed near its entrance. We stopped. Chanthan opened it.

A heap of gold coins! Strewn among them were pearls and coral!

We went down on our haunches and burst into tears.

For a while none of us could talk. We sat on the ground here and there, exhausted, choked with emotion, relieved.

'*Where is Cheera?*'

I leapt up hearing Amma.

We looked frantically among ourselves. We could not find her. Our loud cries brought nothing except echoes from the hill slopes.

Ulakan was telling Chanthan something. When they hurriedly prepared to leave, I joined them.

'She must have gone up there. To the shrine,' Ulakan told me too. We began to climb the hill as fast as we could.

A drizzle. A small shrine in the middle of a mango orchard. Ulakan and Chanthan went in.

I had barely set foot inside the shrine when I tumbled on the ground, struck by lightning. In the steely light, a little girl! Seized by extreme terror, unable to scream, I shut my eyes tight. Aanamala, a mango grove and a little girl rose up in my mind's eye. Here I am, back at the very same place . . .

I saluted her with folded palms, trembling like a leaf.

'Anna,' Ulakan called, stupefied by my transformation. 'What happened to you? This is our Cheera!' He put his arm around her and held her close. I took my eyes off her and gazed at the shrine.

'Do you know, Anna? This shrine is for a little girl who was murdered ruthlessly by Nannan.'

That blew me apart. Inside the shrine was a doll, shaped like a little girl, slumbering on a funeral pyre.

I scrambled out of the shrine somehow and broke into a run. I ran and ran. As fast as my legs could carry me. I did not give ear to the cries of those I left behind. When I tripped and fell, I struggled to get up as fast as I could and ran again. In some places, my leg sank into the muck, but I did not stop. Away, away, away – my mind chanted tirelessly. I ran, walked, lurched, weighed down with fatigue. No, there was no escape for me from that which I had amassed. All that I had thought was buried and gone may rise up from its grave any time to sting me again. I must run away and hide from this very world.

Trudging through the same paths. The same weariness. The same sorrow.

In a few days, I reached Muchiri. That was not to meet anyone. I went straight to the seashore.

*

275

I now stand on the deck of a seafaring ship. It sails on the breast of the boundless sea where the restless waves roll and crash endlessly. My whole life flashes past in my mind's eye one more time. To escape the lashing memories, I fling my gaze towards the opposite shore, far beyond my eyes. But I shut my welling eyes tight, seeing in the reddening horizon a little girl with blazing anklets and a sword that burns a fiery red.

A passing gust of wind shakes hard the ship's masts and soon leaves me behind.

TRANSLATOR'S NOTE

When I first read Manoj Kuroor's *Nilam Poothu Malarnna Naal*, I remembered an experience in a classroom many years ago. Back then, I was a young researcher hoping to grow into a historian, sent by my teachers to a local college in Kottayam to conduct a short introductory workshop on the cultural history of Kerala. Trying to introduce the MA students there to the complexities of Malayalam with its layers of Sanskrit and Tamil, I asked them to translate the Indian English usage 'milk bar'. As expected, the more confident among them piped up: *ksheerasaala*! Drawn, of course, from Sanskrit.

Few alternatives were offered. So I presented to them a Tamil translation of 'milk bar' that I had read on a board on the roadside near the Suchindram temple in the Kanyakumari district of Tamil Nadu: *Paalidam*. *Paal* – milk; *idam* – space. Every single hand in the class went up, and in the snap of a finger! 'That is the correct translation,' everyone agreed.

I still remember the peculiar elation that lingered in the classroom that day. It was as if we had run into something precious utterly by chance, something that had been lost. Something that lay buried under layers and layers of cultural domination, restored to us unexpectedly. Serendipitous! Malayalis write closer to Sanskrit, but speak closer to Tamil. Our Tamil roots still sustain us, yet something keeps us from acknowledging them. But when they burst upon us, we are overcome with joy. Manoj Kuroor's book mesmerised its readers precisely because it suddenly brought to our minds many lost treasures. It is a treasure trove of words which are no longer in Malayalam or which were never there – but could have been, if only new layers had not smothered them so.

There are many aspects of the novel that are utterly fascinating – like the alluring use of the ecological poetics of ancient Tamil poetry to structure the three parts of the novel and the admirable musicality of the three parts, each part almost conforming to a distinct tempo. But no part of it gripped the Malayali reader like its wondrous retrieval of a connection that is so alive in us, if dimmed by cultural conquest and the passing of time.

The translator's challenge, then, would be to recreate that magical elation in the reader. Words had to be chosen carefully. There is a rich sensuousness to the text, which heaves with metaphor and simile, harking back to a time when dry abstraction was not needed so much (but we can see this change slowly, in the last part). Also, this is a world before brahminism gained mastery through the local kings and chieftains; when the 'anthanar' (the brahmins) were yet another group seeking to live their lives alongside other groups of people with their special labours, where 'graded inequality' had not been fully entrenched yet. The translation must therefore be mindful of the moment of history that the text seeks to reimagine. Above all, I think, the translator has also to somehow preserve the wistful and simple beauty of Malayalam prose stripped of the heavy trimmings and enrichments of Sanskrit, but not shorn of all borrowed words.

I thank Sivapriya, my editor, and Manoj, the author, for trusting me with this delicate, beautiful, engrossing and incredibly moving novel. Part of the reason for my accepting this assignment was the chance it offered to work again on a great book with Sivapriya. As for Manoj, I could not have hoped for a better companion on this journey. I thank them both again.

ABOUT THE AUTHOR

Manoj Kuroor is an award-winning poet and professor of Malayalam. He has written poetry, fiction and criticism. He has authored three novels, five collections of poetry, three attakathas (kathakali texts) and written lyrics for films including Shaji N. Karun's *Vanaprastham.*

As a percussionist, Kuroor received basic training in thayampaka, keli and kathakali chenda from his father Kuroor Cheriya Vasudevan Nampoothiri under the supervision of Guru Ayamkudi Kuttappa Marar. He continues to participate in kathakali stage performances while teaching at NSS Hindu College in Changanacherry.

ABOUT THE TRANSLATOR

J. Devika is a historian, feminist, critic and translator. She has written and published in Malayalam and English on gender, politics, literature, social reform and development in Kerala. She translated writings by first-generation feminists in Kerala in *Her Self: Early Writings on Gender by Malayalee Women 1898–1938.* She has also translated contemporary Malayalam writers K.R. Meera, Sarah Joseph, Nalini Jameela, Ambikasuthan Mangad and Unni among others.